Praise for Vivian Arend's
Rocky Mountain Haven

"For those readers who like stories with cowboys, hot love scenes and emotional writing I suggest you start reading this series, you will absolutely love it. Vivian Arend has brought together all of these things plus a slice of Canada to her readers and you do not want to miss it."

~ *Long and Short Reviews*

"I want more Six Pack Brothers!! ...I can't wait for the next story in this series."

~ *Guilty Pleasures Book Reviews*

"If I had to describe this book in one word it would be enchanting. I felt like I was being courted throughout the story... The relationship takes it time to develop and is worth every turn of the page as they blossom from friends to lovers to much more. High praises for *Rocky Mountain Haven*."

~ *Sensual Reads*

"Even though there is some pretty 'hot' sexual activity, *Ricky Mountain Haven* is a warm and loving story and does an excellent job of depicting the true characters of Beth and Daniel... Strap yourself in for some hot phone sex and blistering hot passion!"

~ *Fresh Fiction*

Look for these titles by
Vivian Arend

Now Available:

Granite Lake Wolves
Wolf Signs
Wolf Flight
Wolf Games
Wolf Tracks
Wolf Line

Forces of Nature
Tidal Wave
Whirlpool

Turner Twins
Turn It On
Turn It Up

Pacific Passion
Stormchild
Stormy Seduction
Silent Storm

Six Pack Ranch
Rocky Mountain Heat
Rocky Mountain Haven
Rocky Mountain Desire

Xtreme Adventures
Falling, Freestyle
Rising, Freestyle

Takhini Wolves
Black Gold
Silver Mine

Bandicoot Cove
Exotic Indulgence
Paradise Found

Print Collections
Under the Northern Lights
Under the Midnight Sun
Breaking Waves
Storm Swept
Freestyle
Tropical Desires

Rocky Mountain Haven

Vivian Arend

SAMHAIN
PUBLISHING

Samhain Publishing, Ltd.
11821 Mason Montgomery Road, 4B
Cincinnati, OH 45249
www.samhainpublishing.com

Rocky Mountain Haven
Copyright © 2012 by Vivian Arend
Print ISBN: 978-1-60928-844-0
Digital ISBN: 978-1-60928-561-6

Editing by Anne Scott
Cover by Angela Waters

This book has been previously published and has been revised from its original release.

First Samhain Publishing, Ltd. electronic publication: January 2012
First Samhain Publishing, Ltd. print publication: December 2012

Dedication

For all those women who are brave in ways that people often can't see on the outside—doing what's needed for their children and themselves. Your strength amazes me.

Chapter One

Calgary, Alberta, July

She nursed her drink, waving back at her little sister who was jammed on the dance floor with a hundred other people. Beth tried not to peek at her watch again, instead checking out the myriad faces under the cowboy hats around her. She'd never seen so many boots and buckles in her life. Another round of *Yahoo*s rose into the air from a few well-lubricated throats.

While she appreciated Darleen's attempt at cheering her up and—how had she put it?—"pulling her back to the land of the living", the bar scene had never been her thing.

It definitely wasn't tonight.

One song ended, melding into another ear-shattering rendition of someone done somebody wrong, and Beth held the cool glass of her drink against her temple in the hopes it would slow the throbbing.

"There she is. Hey, Beth, look what I found on the dance floor!" Dar approached the table like a runaway train, dragging not one but two cowboys by the hand. "They're identical twins," she shouted with glee.

Beth raised a brow. They certainly were, from the tops of their Stetsons, past the mischievous grins and the tight faded jeans to the worn shitkickers.

"Well done. Now you need a wandering gypsy and the arctic explorer, and you'll win the scavenger hunt." She offered a hand to the first of the gorgeous specimens. "Beth."

A warm hand clasped her fingers and gave a firm shake while a pair of piercing blue eyes gazed into hers. "Jesse Coleman, that's my brother Joel. I can't help you with an arctic explorer but I might know where there's a gypsy or two."

Beth laughed. "Sorry, but Darleen is a little enthusiastic at times. I'm attempting to keep her centered in reality."

He rearranged a chair and sat in it backward, his mouth-watering smile growing warmer. She sipped her drink. He was hot and kind of cute, but too young for her. Way too young.

"You dancing tonight, Beth, or just exercising your imagination?" Jesse asked. His admiring gaze caused physical reactions she'd missed for far too long. Maybe it *was* time to spread her wings again. She forced herself to take a slow perusal of his body before smiling her approval. His eyes darkened with interest.

That was the kind of response she needed to see.

"Beth doesn't dance since the accident," Darleen piped up before she could answer for herself. "Oops. Sorry, sis. Shut mouth, throw away key."

Beth found both the boys staring and resisted the urge to sigh in exasperation. It's not as if she had planned on keeping it a secret.

She leaned back in her chair and hauled out her leg with its thick supporting brace. "I dance just fine, Darleen, only I take up more room than is available on the floor. You go ahead, I'll watch."

The other twin spoke, adjusting the chairs until there was enough space for them all. "I'm happy to sit for a while. It's been a long day, and the dancing's pretty much worn me out."

Darleen rested on the arm of Joel's chair, her body leaning toward him. Beth coughed then glanced away. Her sister was grown up and could make her own decisions, but she didn't want to be in the know about any specific sexual escapades. From the looks Joel was bestowing on Dar, the potential for something to happen was high.

Besides, Beth had her own agenda tonight, and perhaps the young hotshot seated next to her would be a willing volunteer in her research project. She sipped her drink and checked inwardly to see if she'd had enough to alcohol yet to loosen her inhibitions.

"Why's it called the Six Pack Ranch?" Darleen picked up a conversation they'd obviously started on the dance floor. She now sat firmly in Joel's lap, and Beth blinked at having missed the movement that put her there. "You said the ranch has been around for generations, but six-packs are fairly new."

Jesse laughed easily. "There are so many Colemans in the area, with all the uncles and cousins, folks decided it was easier to stick each of the clans with an additional title. Like our cousins, the Whiskey Creek Colemans—their south boundary runs parallel to the creek. Our spread is officially the SP Ranch after the first initials of the original Coleman brothers who established her, but the smartasses in town decided it stood for Six Pack a few years ago and the new handle stuck."

Beth raised a brow. "The smartasses? Why would they do that? Usually nicknames have some basis in reality."

"You're pretty fixated on reality, aren't you, sweetheart?" Jesse leaned over and took her hand in his, stroking her fingers. If she weren't so sure she might have taught him only a few years earlier in one of her high school math classes, her enjoyment would have been greater. Now she wondered if he was even of legal age to be in the bar. "You're right, there's more. Picture six boys growing up on the ranch. That started the idea. Plus, there's this…"

He rotated smoothly to finish by her side, tugging her close. Yanking up the bottom of his shirt, he slapped her hand onto his abdomen.

Rigid muscles flexed under her palm, and she froze for a second, his hand trapping hers. *Oh God, she'd never felt anything like it before.* Beth involuntarily drew a finger along the well-defined ridges, engrossed by the sensation of individual muscle bundles under the skin. His soft laugh jerked her back to reality—she was fondling a stranger's stomach in public. She snatched her hand away.

She wiggled a finger in his face. "Bad boy."

He laughed and leaned in closer. "I think you like bad boys."

Beth shook her head. He had no idea how much she wanted the exact opposite.

Darleen giggled as Joel nuzzled behind her ear, and Beth knew it was time to make a decision. She snuck a glance from under her lashes to spot Jesse watching the other two at the table jealously, his attention back on her younger sister, and that was all the wake-up call she needed. He might have thought she was amusing to tease, but she was way too old for him. She glanced around the dance floor, a sense of frustration rising. Weren't there any guys over the age of twelve in the room?

"I need to powder my nose." She grabbed her purse and hid her smile as Jesse leapt to his feet to help her. He was a polite thing, wasn't he? If she weren't old enough to have babysat him, it might have been perfect.

With her bulky leg brace, it took some manoeuvring to make it through the crowd to the back of the room. The pulsing beat of the music stirred something inside her, the liquor setting her blood pounding for the first time in forever. The bodies tangling together on the dance floor made her jealous. How long since she'd had someone want her that much? Hands and mouths unable to resist touching, no matter how visible they were to the people around them.

Actually, she'd never had that kind of relationship. She cursed at herself for being a fool and pushed open the door to the washroom harder than she intended, the edge slamming into the wall with a crash. The girls at the sink touching up their lipstick eyed her, and she shook her head in derision, stumbling her way to a stall.

Great, she was freaking out the party animals. The whole bar trip had been a bad idea from the start. As for her secret goal? Obviously getting hot and sweaty was not on the agenda for tonight.

She washed her hands and stared at herself in the mirror. Inside, she felt a million years old, especially after seeing Joel fawn over Dar. On the outside, the news was mixed. Her new short hairstyle suited her dark colouring, the highlights brightening her face, but the tension from the past years had drawn lines at the corners of her eyes and she clearly wasn't twenty anymore. She'd managed to keep her weight stable, even with the bummed-up leg. Her daily runs and the physical high she used to get from them—she missed that. Those times alone had been her only moments of escape from the hell her life had become. In the six months since the accident, there had been no more of that freedom.

Although the worst part of her prison was gone. Hopefully the bastard enjoyed burning in hell like the devil he was.

She made her way back through the crowd. People brushed past, knocking into her, pressing her to and fro until it was difficult to keep her balance. She clung to the railing dividing the dance floor from the rest of the chaos. If she could just catch Dar's eye. Asking for help stuck in her throat, but she'd prefer to beg than end up on her butt on the floor.

An additional body sat at the table in the seat she'd abandoned, and Beth prayed that with three guys vying for her attention, her sister would remember not to leave her behind.

She waved and caught one of the twin's eyes, which one she wasn't sure. He rose to his feet, and she sighed in relief. The idea of fighting her way across the room left her aching. Then the newcomer stood as well and pivoted, his dark eyes examining the room before focusing in her direction.

Her mouth went dry.

Oh my. If she'd thought the twins were good looking, this specimen was dazzling. He was still probably younger than her, but on him the tantalizing features of the other boys had matured, soft edges harder, more pronounced. There was no doubt he was a member of the six-pack they'd spoken about. Whatever else the family raised out on that ranch of theirs, the men were certainly impressive.

She lifted her chin, her pulse quickening as the older cowboy waved his brother down and made his way to her side. People seemed to part before him, and Beth got an eyeful of long, muscular limbs and smooth controlled motion as he approached. Suddenly her little side reason for the trip to the bar slid off the backburner and back into play.

She'd spent the past six months rebuilding her life. While huge holes remained in her world, learning to retake control of her sexuality had finally made it toward the top of the to-do list. After years of dreading her husband's touch, she needed to know if she could stand physical contact with a man. The cowboy she was drooling over looked like a fine volunteer to experiment with—if she could get past her fears and seduce him, or at least attempt to. If she had to call it off in mid-play, this was a safe site. He'd never be able to track her down or figure out her real identity. She'd never have to see him again.

He landed at her side and dipped his head in greeting.

"Daniel Coleman. Can I give you a hand?" He offered his arm and she took it gratefully. The fragrance of his aftershave drifted over and stirred something inside. Her husband had never used any cologne. Claimed a real man didn't need anything but soap and water, and the gift she'd given him had been thrown in the garbage along with a bit of her heart. Now this stranger wore the very scent she'd chosen for Samuel when she was still young and thought she knew what love was. It had to be a good omen.

She was going to take it as a good omen because she needed one.

Back at the table, it was a tight fit. Darleen sat on both twins' laps, their three bodies crowded close together. Beth found herself seated next to Daniel.

The noise level in the bar increased, and Beth gave up trying to listen to the conversation going on three feet in front of her. She'd have to shout to be heard. She turned to see Daniel frown as he watched his brothers.

"Everything okay?"

His face twisted into a wry smile. "Just getting tired of babysitting. Your little sister?"

"Dar doesn't bite. Your boys are safe."

His laugh was real and light. "Then I'll relax. You live in Calgary?"

Did she want to tell him anything about herself? *No.*

God, this was so hard. Here she'd thought that she could at

least handle small talk. She threw back the last mouthful of her drink and changed the topic. The conversation needed to stick to what she wanted to discuss. Somehow she had to lead him into accepting her proposition.

"What's your favourite part of the Stampede?"

He paused and took a long drink of his beer before turning to face her. "I take it you don't want to answer my question."

Damn right she didn't want to tell him any of her personal details. There was no way she would tell him the truth. But the best lies were made of a pinch of reality.

"Daniel, I just want to enjoy myself and take a night to be whoever. Do whatever. I'm not into exchanging life stories. Sorry."

"Understood."

She looked him over closer. A small scar marred the skin beside his right eye, and she touched it without thinking. "You were lucky."

"I deserved it."

Her involuntary reaction to his words was to stiffen in defence. Some triggers remained that were beyond her control. She forced herself to relax, because he didn't mean anything by it. He wasn't talking about her and scars, he was talking about himself.

They were crowded on either side as people forced their way past to reach their seats. His arm draped along the back of her chair brushed her shoulders every now and then. It felt way better than she'd hoped—the riotous fear she had expected remained wonderfully absent. She forced herself to rest her hand on his thigh, trying to make it appear casual, trying not to show how much effort it took to not flinch away. He rocked, making his leg shift. Firm muscles pressed against the jean material, and she sucked in a quick breath, wondering what he was about to do. Heat radiated upward, and her core tightened. The twins took off, dragging her sister back to the dance floor.

She leaned closer under the pretence of wanting to be heard without shouting. Her nose itched as it struck the short hairs behind his ear. The scent of his skin, so different from her husband's, gave her courage. That wonderful mixture of man and aftershave, slightly rough, slightly wild. Her nipples tightened, and between her legs her body ached.

Okay, those were good signs. The whole libido thing wasn't broken beyond repair.

"Dar's going to have a hard time picking which one she likes better, you know."

His shoulder pressed against her body as he leaned back, twisting his head to the side to reach her ear. He sighed, the warm air tickling her skin. "Will you go ballistic if I tell you they're going to try their best to get her to pick them both?"

She choked before pulling back to look him in the eye. "Hello?"

Daniel grimaced. "They won't force anything, but they enjoy having one girl between the two of them. I know it's not your usual situation, and I'm not saying it's the norm in my family or anything. But they've always been like that and so far I haven't heard any complaints."

She sat shocked for a moment, turning to watch the slow dance taking place on the floor. There were more than enough bodies to explain why the three of them had to be dancing so close, but sure enough, the younger Colemans had trapped Darleen on two sides. Beth debated for a moment, her heart pounding. *What if...*

No, she couldn't start imaging what if her sister suddenly had to deal with two overly aggressive men. Not all males were like Samuel. If Dar wanted to cut loose tonight, hell if her big sister was going to stop her. Life was short, and she should take what fun she could.

"More power to them." She said it quietly, but she knew he'd heard. He relaxed, his arm brushing her again. On to other important issues. It was now or never because she was one second away from fleeing. "What about you, Daniel?"

She pressed her hand against his thigh, letting the weight of it linger. If she had the courage, she would have been even more forward, but that was impossible. This was as deliberate as she could get.

She held her breath, waiting for his reaction. Would he ridicule her? Brush her aside?

He stared for a full minute and heat crept up her neck. It was one thing to act the hussy and another to pull it off. *Fine.* The whole plan had been rotten from the word go. She dropped her eyes and retreated. She was withdrawing her hand when he grasped her wrist, locking it in place with a steely grip. She bit her lip to hide the whimper of fear that wanted to escape, but his grasp, while it held her immobile, remained gentle.

He leaned in. "I'm not usually the type for this kind of thing, but if you're asking for something on the wild side, hell yeah, I can oblige you. I don't know why someone like you isn't getting well taken care of already. For tonight, if you want me to make you happy, I'll do my damnedest."

She swallowed hard. It was a trap. No escape. Controlling. Her heart fluttered with fear, and she closed her eyes to concentrate. Okay, this was why she was making the attempt in public. It was safe. All she had to do was say stop and everything would be over.

His grip loosened, and he stroked his fingers over hers, a fleeting touch with the back of his hand caressing her skin. The coarse hair on his arm tickled her as he moved past her wrist, his body tight to hers, his lips hovering over her ear. The loud beat of music pounded the room. The table. Her body. It had to be the music—it wasn't her pulse making her shake so hard.

The warmth of his breath brushed her neck, sending a shiver trickling over her skin. "You sure—completely sure— about this?" He drew back and cupped her chin in his hand, supporting her without locking her in place. "I've been around a lot of animals in my lifetime, and I know when one's skittish. You may have the most come-hither attitude and sexy stare I've ever seen, but your body is telling a different story."

Beth wiggled but refused to drop her gaze. She had to bluff her way through this. She was a grown woman taking back control of her life. It was the first step and she could handle it. *Couldn't she?*

His gaze descended her body, an intimate caress without physical contact. "What's it going to be? Do I grab my brothers and we pop you and your sister in a cab so you get safely home? Or do you really want a little company tonight? Shoot straight, I won't accept a lie."

Beth licked her lips, and his eyes darkened, his stare fixed on her mouth. She stuttered for a second, then swallowed and took a deep breath. Part of the truth burst out.

"I need this. I need to know..." She couldn't maintain eye contact anymore and buried her face against his shoulder. *Shoot.* It had been a stupid idea to begin with, and there was no getting around it. Now she sounded desperate, which she was, but acknowledging it was brutally difficult.

He'd turned out to be exactly the kind of person she needed for a one-night stand, compassionate and caring. Something inside her cringed with disgust at herself. Using him as an experiment felt dirtier than when she'd first come up with the idea.

He stood and helped her to her feet.

"What are you doing?"

"I thought we could dance." He wove through the masses, leading away from the crowded floor toward the bathrooms. There was a small landing kitty-corner to the ladies' room door, and he guided her there before pulling her into his arms and wrapping her close. She hid her face again, fear and rising desire fighting in her body. They were only steps away from the crowd. A constant stream of women passed by. If he frightened her, she'd have help in an instant.

She relaxed a tiny bit and let her arms snake around his torso.

"Hmm, that's better. You're not going to bolt on me, are you?"

Beth shook her head. "Feels nice."

He swayed with her, every inch in contact. Her cheek rested on his collar, and his fragrance filled her head. Why was it that the smell of this man turned her on so much?

His heartbeat—it vibrated against her chest. He adjusted them, somehow bringing her closer until they were lined up, his erection nudging her belly. "I need to hear what you want, Beth. If it's a dance, I'm happy. If more, you need to say the word."

Oh God, he shifted his hands on her back, caressing, teasing. She sucked in air as if it were courage. "I want something. I don't know what to tell you."

He lifted her face to his, their bodies still swaying, hips touching intimately. Slowly, with lots of time for her to retreat, he lowered his head and brushed their lips together. A single touch. Chaste. When he retreated, she followed him without intending to.

A bright light shone in his dark eyes as he examined her

face. "That was something. Was it enough?"

She took it as a positive sign that she definitely wanted more. "No."

"So tell me."

It was the hardest thing, to say the word. "Please."

He had a wicked smile. She'd noticed his good looks, but the smile turned his whole face into sin incarnate.

"You're having trouble articulating, darling. How about I offer you multiple choices. You look like the type who enjoys options."

He kissed her again. Light. Fleeting. Behind them, the bathroom door opened and closed but Beth barely noticed. There could have been an audience circling them, and she wouldn't have cared.

"You want a kiss?" He brushed a thumb over her lips and brought it back to his mouth, licking the moisture from the pad. "Hmm, you taste good. You want me to kiss you for real? Like a man kisses his woman? Or are you happy with more of the kind of pecks you give a neighbour at a church picnic?"

She swore she spoke aloud. She was sure her lips moved, but the deafening buzz in her ears outweighed the sound of her own voice. Daniel gave her another sexier-than-sin grin and came back for a third pass. She closed her eyes and hoped like hell she'd said door number one.

He gripped her tighter and lifted her, heavy brace and all, and she gasped in surprise. Then he tore the rest of the air from her lungs as he consumed her. Crushing their lips together, he thrust his tongue into her mouth and took control. She waited for panic to descend, but all that hit was a heavy pulse between her legs and the urgent desire to drop to the floor and rip off his clothes. She opened to him, accepted his demands. Clung to his neck and writhed shamelessly against him. He held her, cupping her by the ass and pushing forward until the cold wall met her shoulders. He leaned into her, supporting her with his torso and hands, pulsing his hips with small movements so the ridge of his erection ground against the apex of her mound where blood beat with an insane tempo.

He tasted fantastic. Clean and fresh, the hint of hops on his tongue from the beer, but beyond that, nothing but heat and passion. Tingles spread across her belly from the constant pressure on her clit. When he lowered her to the floor, she whimpered, suddenly fearful he'd leave her at this point, frustrated and all alone again with nothing but her own hand to bring her over the edge.

He caged her against the wall, his lips brushing her ear. He snuck his hand between their bodies until he cupped her breast. "Time for two more options. You want me to touch you over your clothes or put my fingers on your bare flesh?"

He licked her earlobe and tugged her blouse, pulling it loose from the waist of her skirt.

This was insane. She'd gone insane. This was no longer an exercise to discover if she could again bear physical contact with a man. It was a torture method to see how much her body could take before she exploded from the mere thought of a caress.

"Skin." It was the only possible choice.

Whisper light, seductively slow. Inch by inch his hand crept up her waist, strumming the curve of her ribs gently like piano keys, lifting the bottom edge of her bra and forcing it out of his way. He cupped her, his palm calloused and rough but so tender and careful she shivered. He distracted her with strokes of his tongue against hers as his fingers plucked her nipple to a hard peak.

"God, you're driving me mad." He rolled the sensitive tip

between thumb and forefinger and a piercing flash shot straight between her legs.

"More." Beth ached. It wasn't enough to have confirmation she could be touched. She wanted to come, and she wanted Daniel to be the one who brought her over the peak. It had been too long, and something in this man made her think he'd understand if she told him what she truly needed. Why.

"Get a room!"

Laughter burst behind them. Daniel twisted, covering her with his body, protecting her from the giggling girls exiting the bathroom and traipsing back onto the dance floor.

A cold flush descended. What was she thinking? Groping in a hallway with a stranger. All the passion she'd felt, the sense of being truly alive, drained away like air from a balloon. She struggled upright and fumbled to put herself back in order—her bra, her blouse. He helped, his hands remaining careful and slow, redoing the buttons that had slipped open, tucking her hair behind her ear.

"Beth. Don't. Don't start thinking this was a mistake."

She glanced up in astonishment. "How did you...?"

He brushed a hand over her cheek and she stilled again, her skin burning hot. "Your only mistake was thinking a short encounter in a back hall would be enough. I'm not that type." He shook his head, his eyes fixed on hers. "I don't think you're that type either. Not really."

She hesitated, then nodded with reluctance. He deserved that much honesty. It was all she was willing to give.

"Let me get to know you better. We've got the chemistry. I'd like to find out who you are when you're not trying to be someone else."

Every word drove another nail into her guilty conscious.

"Sure. Let's go back to the table. Darleen must be wondering where I am."

He kissed her once more and she took it eagerly. Trying to store up the memory of his taste, the way he tugged his fingers through her hair just right. None of the fear she'd expected was there. When he drew back, she had to fight to keep tears from falling. He had no idea, but he'd helped remind her she was free. Samuel had tied her in knots, and Daniel had cut some of the remaining cords that held her bound.

They headed to the table, but their previous space was filled with strangers. Beth spotted Darleen waiting beside the bar door, wearing a frown so deep it was almost comical.

"Shoot. Looks like there was trouble in paradise."

Daniel pointed to the far side of the room where Jesse and Joel tossed back beers at the long bar counter. "Double shoot. Jackasses. I'll whoop their butts if they—"

She shook her head. "Knowing Dar, it's just as easily her fault. It's only a night out on the town."

He turned her in his arms. "It's more than a night on the town for me. I like you, Beth. There's something about you..."

His gaze traced her hair and she flushed. She hadn't intended the evening to finish this way.

Daniel pulled out his wallet and handed her a card. "It's for the family business, but my contact numbers are on there. You can email me, or phone." He handed her an extra card. "Write your number on the back for me."

He pulled her close, and she used his chest as a solid base to scribble her name. Beth Jackson. Jotted down a number. He took the card and tucked it away, his dark gaze burning a hole in her conscience. "I'll call you a cab."

She held up a hand, refusing his offer. "We have a car.

We're fine."

Dar flounced out the door and Beth rolled her eyes. With the rest of her dilemmas, she had no energy to deal with her temperamental little sister. She took one last look at her cowboy, wishing things could be different.

"Thanks, Daniel. It was great meeting you."

He brushed her cheek with a kiss. "I'll call you in the morning. I'd love to take you for coffee."

She smiled and stepped away, the relentless noise and the situation making her head and heart hurt. "That would be great," she lied.

The cool night air brushed her face, refreshing after the heat of the bar, and she sucked in a calming breath. Dar brought the car around, and Beth manoeuvred herself into the passenger seat, the leg brace frustrating and cumbersome.

"Where the hell were you?" Darleen griped. "I've been wanting to leave forever."

Beth dropped her head against the rest and groaned. She was sexually frustrated, her leg ached, and she really didn't want to listen to whining right now. "I thought you were busy. With two guys."

Darleen had the grace to look embarrassed. "Yeah, well, they were nice enough. Then one of the Stampeders asked me to dance. I mean, one of the linebackers from the professional football team? I had to say yes, and when I got back, the guys had left."

Stupid child.

"You went and danced with someone else and expected them to wait for you?" Darleen didn't say anything. Beth rolled down her window and let the sounds of the city streets soothe her soul. "Can't have it all, girl."

Darleen flicked a hand in her direction. "Whatever. It was still fun, I guess. How about you? Their older brother was hot. Did you hit it off with him?"

A lingering pulse beat between her legs. Did they hit it off? *Oh sweet Jesus.* "Yes."

"You going to see him again?"

Beth stared at the card he'd given her. She'd been clutching it like a lifeline. The dark expression in Daniel's eyes scared her yet gave her hope, and for one moment she hesitated.

No. It was time for a total break. She tore the card into tiny little pieces so she wasn't tempted to try and recover the numbers. "Nope. I'm leaving town with the boys in two weeks. Making a new start, and I don't need any baggage in the shape of male stalkers, thanks very much. Been there, burnt the T-shirt."

"Guys aren't all like Samuel, you know. There are good ones out there."

Was Daniel one of the good ones? Beth dropped the scraps into the trash bag and adjusted her leg. "Enough. I want to go home. Mom's bringing the boys back in the morning, so it's not as if we can sleep in."

She stared out the window and wished more than anything Daniel were the one taking her home and tucking her into bed.

Chapter Two

Rocky Mountain House, Alberta, August

"What do you mean I can't get keys to the apartment? I've got one week to settle in before school starts. I need the key."

The owner of her rental complex leaned back on his beat-up truck and shrugged in slow motion. Beth wanted to scream. She wanted to kick something. Most of all she wanted to start unloading the boxes she'd brought with her from Calgary before she completely ran out of steam. Her boys had crawled into the front seat of the moving van, three sets of eyes gazing down as they waited in silence.

"Sorry, ma'am, but see, that's what I'm trying to tell you. There was a fire a couple of nights ago. Far end of the complex, but the fire marshal shut down the whole place until the wiring can be inspected."

She tapped her good foot. If he would talk a little faster, the conversation might be done by the end of the weekend. "Are there any other apartments for rent in town?"

A slow shift of the shoulders. "There were. Until yesterday. All the other occupants of the apartment house had to find alternative arrangements too. I think just about everything available got snapped up."

The throbbing in her temples couldn't be good. She rubbed her fingers against her forehead. Now what? Head back to

Calgary and beg her parents to let her stay with them again? Drive three hours twice every day to get to school once her teaching position began?

"I'll have to check into a hotel or motel." She couldn't afford it, but... "Do you know which one would be the cheapest for a long-term stay?"

The old codger raised a brow. "Well, you could try the motel, but if you give me a minute, I bet we can do you one better. Since it's partly my fault you're in this mess." He gestured at the U-Haul. "You need a place to dump all that anyway. Won't fit at a motel, I'm guessing."

He hauled out a cell phone, and she turned her back to stop the hysterical giggles that wanted to rise up and overtake her. The incongruity of his worn overalls and the shiny new phone was too much to handle when she stood on the verge of a breakdown.

"Mommy. Are we lost?"

She smiled at Nathan, his blond head poking out from the window of the truck. "No, we're in the right spot, only there's a mix-up. We'll get it figured out."

Lance popped up beside him. "Are we still going to live here? It smells."

Oh Lord. "Yes, we're moving here. You're going to school here. I'm teaching here. Nothing has changed since the last time you asked, twenty minutes ago. And it doesn't smell any worse than your bedroom before we cleaned it up to get ready to move."

Nathan laughed at him and Lance stuck out his tongue. Robbie forced his way between his brothers, all three of them hanging precariously from the window. "I have to go pee."

Beth sighed. She glanced at her erstwhile landlord who was still talking on the phone. He laughed at something then motioned at her, flashing a thumbs-up while he continued to yatter. A 7-Eleven across the street caught her eye, and she motioned for the boys to back up.

"Bathroom break for everyone. I'll buy you a Slurpee, then I expect you to stay quiet until I get this little issue solved. We'll hit a park as soon as we can, okay?"

They clambered down, and she pulled them in tight for a hug. Life had been hellishly tough at times lately, but these dirty, smiling faces made it all worthwhile. She waved a hand at Mr. Jordon then pointed across the street. He never broke stride in his discussion, which now seemed to be about feeding tomato plants with fish fertilizer to get the best yield. She really hoped somewhere in the conversation he had managed to find them a temporary home.

They recrossed the street ten minutes later, three contented boys clinging to sweet frosty drinks. Didn't take much to make her crew happy.

Mr. Jordon grinned, pride filling his face. "I talked to my friend, Mike. He said there were no troubles with you taking possession of Grampa Peter's homestead for a bit. His oldest sons have been living in it, but there's plenty of room at home for them temporarily like. You're even welcome to rent the place with the furniture if you need it. Six months sound good? I'll promise you space back here at the end of that time since we weren't ready when we promised."

"A house?" Hope brightened her weary load. What she wouldn't give for a house to live in, instead of an apartment. It would be so much better for the boys, but she knew exactly what her expenses were going to be, and the cost for a house was probably out of reach. "How much does he want for rent?"

Mr. Jordon snorted. "He didn't want a damn thing, but since I figured you'd have issues with that, he said to tell you he'd take what you were going to pay me. No first and last. Just get him the money when you can. Any furniture you want to use, you use. Anything you don't want, there's an outbuilding to store things in." He eyed her leg brace. "Who's helping you unload the truck?"

"We are." Lance spoke up. He'd been hanging back politely but marched forward to stand wide-legged in front of her, his fists resting on his hips. Her heart ached at the sight. Only eight, and he was already trying to take care of her. "We're Mommy's helpers."

Mr. Jordon nodded sagely. "And mighty fine ones too, I bet. But you see, I know a few other young men, strapping strong fellows like yourself. Perhaps I can get them to help as well. You know, so you can show them how it's done."

Lance's face lit up and Beth breathed out slowly. It looked as if her insane idea to take her family to a place with a quieter pace of life might work after all.

She smiled at the older man. "I'd like to see the house before I make any commitments, but I really do appreciate your help."

He laughed, peeling himself off his truck and yanking the door open. "Didn't do nothing. Tell you what, you follow me. We'll take a spin out to the Peter's place. The Colemans are all working right now, so we won't be disturbing anyone. If you're happy with the place, we'll come back and get you put up for the night at the hotel. That'll give the boys time to clear out their things, and tomorrow I'll get my grandsons to help your fine moving team get you settled."

Beth nodded at another of the adults she recognized from the *Meet the Teacher* night she'd attended a week earlier.

Settling into the community had gone far better than she'd expected, with early September the usual whirl of commotion. Lance and Nathan loved their teachers in the small elementary school, and Robbie's kindergarten class seemed to spend more time outdoors than inside, which was exactly what the active little boy needed.

Nathan tugged at her shirt. "There's Jimmy. Can I go with him?" He was away before she could confirm or deny his request, tackling his friend, the two of them rolling on the ground like puppies.

The other mom smiled in greeting. "Hi, Beth. They are excited today, aren't they? I can take your boys with me to the kids' play area, if you're okay with that." Lance bounced on the spot, eager to go as well but unwilling to leave without permission.

Another joy she'd discovered living in the smaller community. Never before had she felt comfortable leaving her boys in someone else's company. Since she'd always been home, they'd never gone to day care in Calgary. Samuel had discouraged any regular playgroups. She'd never wanted to get too close to anyone and have too many questions asked. Here in Rocky Mountain House people went out of their way to say hello, to get to know the boys and offer help.

She gave her assent, and the older boys roared off like airplanes to the colouring contest and penny carnival areas of the community picnic. Robbie clung to her hand as they walked the fairgrounds, the crowds of families racing past and the clatter of the music making him shier than usual.

"Well, if it isn't my lovely neighbour and her escort. Hey, Robbie boy, you enjoying yourself?"

Beth smiled at the older man as he adjusted his crutches so he could bend over and ruffle her son's hair. Her temporary landlord had turned out to be nothing short of an angel. He and his eldest son, Blake, had cleared their things from the Peter's house and arranged for storage for the household goods she didn't need.

Now a month later, she was even more grateful as she watched her sons thrive. They needed this. In fact, she needed it too—a chance to see there were good people in the world.

"Mike, it's good to see you. Is Marion here as well?"

He shook his head. "She's feeling under the weather. But you need to drop by the house soon and join us for dinner like you promised. Marion thinks you're avoiding us."

Beth lifted a brow. "We'd love to come by, but if you remember, a couple days before we were scheduled to drop in you decided to play chicken with a moose." She pointed to his cast. "How is your leg?"

"It'll be fine. The boys are taking care of the harvest, so I'm sitting back and being a man of leisure this fall." He winked. "You and me, we could enter the three-legged race and still be a leg short."

They laughed, their injuries another common bond between them.

Robbie tugged on Mike's one good pant leg. "How do chickens and moose play together?"

A serious expression crossed the older man's face. "Excellent question. How about I explain while you enjoy some picnic food?" He glanced at Beth for permission and she nodded. A bit of positive male interaction in Robbie's life was exactly what he needed. "We'll meet you for coffee and dessert later."

Beth wandered, working her way around the fair grounds. The measured gait she found most comfortable with her brace wasn't as noticeable amongst the slow-moving crowds. The bright sunshine lit not only the sky but some of the dark places in her heart. The pace of life here in Rocky was slower. The people, while not all friendly, were a lot more open to talking to her on the street corner than in Calgary where she'd barely known her neighbours after ten years of living in the same house. The sense of being an outsider hadn't struck her yet, perhaps because she'd stepped into the school system and had an instant group of associates. Some of her co-workers were locals who had returned to teach in their alma mater. Some were newer teachers putting in time at a smaller school in the hopes of transferring back to the big city.

And her. Wondering where she fit for the long term.

Working full-time outside the house for the first time in years was physically draining, especially with the extra weight of the brace and her leg injury still giving her grief. The boys were a handful, brimming with energy and excitement. They were easier to deal with now that she didn't have her husband's exacting demands to meet as well.

She sat by the outdoor stage to listen to the local band and let her mind wander. Her husband—being free from his overbearing expectations and his downright emotional cruelty made every day worthwhile, no matter how exhausted she was when she fell into bed. The pain in her leg and hip were nothing compared to the pain he'd caused in their lives on a regular basis.

No, life was good. She had little to complain about.

If the house occasionally creaked at night and frightened her, or the wind blew around the porch with a lonely sound, she was better off by herself than letting her family continue to suffer under the hands of a tyrant.

She closed her eyes and listened to the music. The band played a few country songs, followed by some hard rock. The electric guitar was slightly out of tune, and the occasional louder dissonance brought a smile to her face. The heat of the sun pulled her into drowsing, laughter and voices and music melding together into a far more relaxing lullaby than the clatter of the city. Beth breathed deep. Even the smells surrounding her felt right.

A long time later a clanging bell shook her from her tranquil rest. The community people congregated around the food tent for coffee and dessert. She ambled over, reluctant to lose the relaxed state she'd achieved. Lance and Nathan raced up, faces glowing with excitement to chatter about all they'd done. Other boys gathered with them, pushing and wrestling good-naturedly. The adults in the lineup worked together to calm and seat the unruly crew at the long tables. Pies and cakes before them, the clamour of little-boy voices vanished as their mouths filled.

"Amazing, isn't it?" Mike patted Robbie on the back, and he scrambled between his brothers, eager to attack his plate. "The only time our house ever got quiet when my boys were little was during meals."

Beth smiled. "I don't mind the noise. Especially the laughter."

Mike shook his head. "Well, they laughed, but with six boys, the shouting is the thing I remember most."

She frowned as they headed over to another table to grab coffee. "Six? I've only met two—Blake and Travis. I didn't know you had six children."

"Are you serious? I thought you'd have met them all by now. It's not that big a town. Although, they're not round the school that much since they're all older. Come on, I can introduce you to two more. They're right up here."

He gestured her forward. Ahead, standing behind the coffee

table, were familiar-looking identical twins. She frowned as she tried to place their faces. Maybe she had seen them around town. They looked somewhat like their older brother, Blake.

One of them glanced up and smiled, a devastating and seductive grin, and memory rolled over her. *Oh no.* It was the pair from her disastrous bar adventure back in July.

"Beth, I'd like to introduce Jesse and Joel, my youngest boys."

Twin number one grinned wider. "I know you. You decided to try and find the gypsies?"

She swallowed hard and mindlessly accepted the cup of coffee he offered. *No.* No, this was not real. "You live here?"

He nodded, his brows rising. "And someone else lives here too you might be interested in. He was mighty vocal when a certain phone number turned out to be disconnected."

Beth froze in dismay. This couldn't be happening. Not when she'd started to set down roots. Could one night of foolishness really ruin her plans?

"Speak of the devil..." Jesse's bright blue eyes stared past her shoulder, and she cringed inside. She held the coffee cup like a shield and rotated on the spot to see her handsome cowboy approaching. His gaze met hers, and the expression on his face changed in an instant. The friendly smile vanished, shock replacing it, followed by a tinge of anger.

Her cup slipped from her trembling fingers as fear and regret took control.

Chapter Three

Daniel forced his feet to continue moving even as his brain scrambled to recover from his shock. She looked different than he remembered. Somehow happier, more content, at least until the panic set in. Her face had gone completely white, and she trembled before him, her spilt coffee cup at her feet. She rubbed her fingers together.

"Beth, you okay?" Mike reached for her, but Daniel moved quicker. He had no idea where in the hell she'd come from, but there was no way she was getting away again. He scooped the cup from the ground then turned her, one arm loosely around her waist as he guided her to a nearby chair at one of the long tables arranged on the lawn.

"Sit down before you fall down." She shivered, and he barked over his shoulder at his brother. "Pour her another cup of coffee and add a couple of sugars to it."

"I don't need anything. I'm fine." Her gaze darted around them, and Daniel finally realized she was embarrassed by the attention they were drawing. He rose from where he'd squatted beside her, seating himself on the next chair.

"Of course you're fine. Now, can I get you a piece of pie to go with your coffee?" They could pretend this was normal meeting at a picnic until everyone found something else to stare at. He would wait until he got her alone to wring some answers from her pretty lips.

He'd been surprised how much her deception had upset him. Somehow he'd imagined she'd felt an inkling of what he'd experienced that night in the bar. He could have sworn there was a connection between them. When he'd discovered the number she gave him was out of service, and there was no Beth Jackson in the phone book, he should have simply laughed and written the scene off as an interesting encounter.

Only, he couldn't. She'd haunted him. Her confused eyes full of passion and fear, her stubborn determination to try to seduce him. Hell, the only reason he'd even gone out that night was because the twins had taunted him to the point of insanity. Meeting her—he thought it had been his reward, especially when she softened in his arms. When she switched from trying to be a sex kitten into a warm submissive woman, curved in all the right places. He thought he'd found someone he really wanted to get to know better.

He accepted two cups of steaming liquid from Jesse, motioning his brother to step away and leave them alone. Mike watched with curiosity for a moment before tapping her on the shoulder. "You relax for a bit, Beth, I'll deal with the boys. Okay?"

She nodded rapidly, her eyes focused down at the table. They sat quietly for a few minutes, the curious onlookers slowly wandering off in search of action.

Daniel coughed. "This is a tad awkward, isn't it?"

Beth lifted her gaze to meet his. "I'm so embarrassed."

He shrugged. "People drop coffee cups all the time. Not a worry."

A laugh burst from her lips, and he enjoyed the way her whole face changed when she smiled. "You're a surprise. That's all I can say."

It was mutual. He stared over the picnic ground. Activities

were breaking up, and out in public probably wasn't the best place for the discussion he wanted to have anyway.

"I assume you're living in town?" *Hell.* There was another possibility, although she seemed to be alone. "Or are you here visiting someone?"

There was a moment's hesitation before she spoke. "I live here. Moved in the middle of August to start a job at the high school."

Oh yeah, that was what he wanted to hear. He pushed back his chair.

"Can I give you a ride home?" He wanted her alone to continue the conversation he'd planned on having two months earlier.

"Daniel!" A swarm of little arms choked the life out of him, and he pulled back to grin at the three troublemakers he'd been watching over lately.

"Hey, guys. Was the picnic fun?" They had dirt on their jeans, grass in their hair and the littlest one had smears of chocolate on his face. "You look as if you had a good time."

Three voices all sang out in unison, and he could barely understand them.

"I hit the target a zillion times!"

"I wanted another corncob, but they ran out."

"Can we go swimming again?"

Daniel laughed. "Slow down. One at a time and..." He froze. Holy shit, he was a stupid son of gun. He stared at Beth in shock. "These are *your* boys?"

Her frown was firmly in place. "Lance, how do you know Daniel?"

The oldest boy went completely silent and kicked at the ground. "Umm..."

Oh hell. "You boys never told your mama you were playing down at the swimming hole, did you?"

From her reaction it was the first she'd heard of the place, ever. Two bright spots rose on her cheeks, the rest of her face suddenly gone white. Her lips tightened. "You mean they've been by the water without me knowing?"

She swallowed hard and wavered in her seat. He could see guilt and fear, in her eyes. Damn it, he shouldn't have assumed just because he and his brothers had spent their summers running wild on the ranch that everyone would be okay with that for their own kids.

Beth spoke firmly to her sons. "We'll talk about this on the way home. Come on, it's time to go."

Daniel rose with her, steadying her when she landed on a rough section of grass. After all this time, she was living not more than five minutes from his front door. His mind reeled.

"I'll walk along with you."

"That's not necessary—"

Mike swung past, moving on his crutches far faster than a man his age should. He blocked their path and grinned at Beth. "I take it you've met my middle boy before."

Daniel stared off into the distance to hide his face as Beth responded. His father was being a stubborn ass. It wasn't like him to get in the way and be so curious about the women his boys took an interest in. What was he playing at?

"Daniel, if you've got a minute, could you go and make sure the heating coil is turned on around the water pipes at the Peter's house? It's getting colder, and I'd hate to forget to do it before it freezes."

"I can do that," Beth insisted. "Just tell me where to look and…"

Mike shook his head. "I'm not letting a lady crawl under the house. Daniel knows where it is. It'll only be a minute's work, right?"

"Yes, sir." Daniel watched Beth closely. He wanted to talk to her, needed to talk, but if it was too much today, he'd back off.

After all, he knew where to find her.

She stared up from under her lashes and his body tightened. She may have been surprised to see him, but the interest they'd shared before—it still seemed to be there. Beth guided her boys toward the parking lot, the three tykes suitably subdued.

"I'll meet you there," Daniel called after her. He'd love to be a fly in the car and hear what the boys had to say about the swimming hole. Smart kids, even if they were in a heap of trouble at the moment.

He followed her van back toward the house where he'd lived until a few weeks ago. They passed the original ranch house where he currently slept. Daniel loved the layout of the entire SP Ranch. His great-grandpa and his brother had planned well when they had set up the place. Of the two homesteads, what they still called the Peter's house was slightly smaller. It had been built after the two bachelor brothers had gotten married and started families within a year of each other. The second house stood on the other side of the coulee and creek. The layout had given both families privacy, and yet easy access to the barns and storage for their joint field equipment.

Years later, the Peter's house had provided a wonderful location for the oldest boys to get out from under their parents' roof without moving into town. At twenty-six, Daniel had been batching it with Blake and Matt for the past eight years. It felt awfully strange to have moved back into the home of his youth.

On an impulse, he turned down a side gravel road that led

to the back of the barns. He left his truck there and strode through the trees, crossing the small footbridge to access the other side of the property. He made it to the Peter's house just as Beth pulled in. The boys poured out of the van and raced for the door.

"Night, Daniel." Three sets of hands waved as the kids shot up the wide porch stairs to disappear in to the house.

He laughed and turned to face Beth. "I see you've been living in the country long enough you're not locking your doors anymore."

She opened her mouth then closed it tight, wrinkling her nose for a moment. "You're right. I hadn't even thought about that."

When she moved slowly toward the house, he hurried to offer his arm.

"Your leg sore?" he asked.

She shook her head. "Just not looking forward to doing the 'Mom speech'. I decided to save it until we got home so I could concentrate on the road."

Damn, no wonder the kids ran off so fast. "For what it's worth, the creek is a pretty harmless place. It's not very deep, and usually a whole lot of mud. I think I caught them the first time they were down there, and I've been keeping an eye out for them ever since, so they've been safe."

"Thank you for that." She opened the door. "Good night."

"I'll wait here once I'm done with my chore, until you've got a minute to talk."

Beth clutched the doorknob so hard her fingers went white. "I have to put the boys to bed."

"No troubles. I've got nowhere I've got to be." Panic flashed in her eyes again, but he refused to back down. He wasn't going to push this too far, but now that he'd found her—she could run, but she couldn't hide. He dipped his head, maintaining eye contact until she had to pull her gaze away.

Three little faces stared upward, lips quivering. She barely had the strength to finish her lecture on staying safe and making sure Mom knew where they were at all times without breaking into a smile.

"We're sorry, Mommy."

She hugged them close. Now that her heart had slowed from the fear of having them near the water alone, she understood the attraction. Although, they hadn't been unsupervised—her mysterious stranger had been there. Daniel had managed to tangle himself into her life whether she wanted him there or not.

"Okay, guys. I know you're excited from the picnic, but it's time to start slowing things down. I want all of you in the tub, then we can read together before bed."

The boys raced off to the bathroom, voices raised in energetic shouts. Beth breathed a contented sigh until she remembered Daniel waited on her deck. What in the world was she going to do?

She placed a trembling hand on the back door. There was no unwind button she could push. No way to make the past disappear. He was probably stubborn enough if she didn't go out he'd sit there all night like he'd threatened. She sucked in her courage and pressed the door open.

The porch boards squeaked, announcing her approach, and he looked up from where he'd settled on the old-fashioned swing.

He hesitated before speaking, sincerity clear in his tone. "You've got awesome kids. I'm sorry again about the swimming-hole thing. It never crossed my mind you didn't know."

She waved his confession away. "I'm mortified I didn't figure out where they were disappearing to. I should have kept much better tabs on their whereabouts, and I'm grateful you had an eye on them."

He stood and peeked in the window. "Will you need to go and get them into bed?"

"They'll start on their own, but they'll get distracted soon."

Daniel smiled. "I think my mama used to say it was like trying to herd cats to get us all in bed on time. I won't keep you long, but..." He reached for her hand, threading his fingers between hers. She swallowed hard. Oh Lord, it felt so good and scared her mindless at the same time. She stood as still as a statue in spite of her pounding heart.

"I'd like to see you, Beth."

She bit her lip. "I don't think that's a good idea."

He turned over her fingers, his thumb brushing the groove on her ring finger that was slowly disappearing. After ten years of wearing her wedding band, the sign was still there, even though the ring was not. "You're not married."

She shook her head. "He's gone." He raised a brow, and she had to say it, knowing the confusion not speaking plainly would cause. "He's dead. He died in the accident that injured my leg."

Her throat went tight. Images flashed through her mind, the icy road, the glaring lights. The pain.

The guilt.

His fingers stopped. "I'm sorry."

He moved to pull away, and impulsively she resisted, maintaining a hold on his hand. Damn her indecision.

"It's...okay. We were having troubles when he died, and I'm not grieving for him. Not really. I just don't think it's a great idea for you and me..." She couldn't speak. What she wanted and what she should do—why was it so hard to know which was which?

He squeezed her fingers then let go and paced away. "There's a whole lot I think you're not saying right now. That's fine. I'm still the man you met one night while you were in a drunken state and you don't know me."

"I wasn't drunk."

He chuckled and her face heated. "We call that liquid courage around here, darling, and you had some. I want you to know I was serious back then when I said I was interested in you. I'm even more interested, knowing you're not a city girl living in some high-rise apartment hours away from me."

"Maybe I'm not staying."

"Then maybe while you're here, we should spend some time together. I'm a good man, Beth. I'm not talking about taking over your life. I'm saying you intrigue me and you make my body ache. I think our attraction is something worth exploring."

He moved closer. Her pulse pounded, and she tilted her head involuntarily to keep their eyes in contact.

Another step.

"I want to kiss you," he growled. Their bodies were close enough their heat meshed, and a gasp of need escaped her throat. "Do you want to kiss me?"

Oh God. "I shouldn't."

"But do you want to?"

Desire and being responsible warred within her. Accepting his touch tonight would make it all that much harder to turn him down the next time.

He pressed closer yet, and their torsos connected, his groin rubbing her belly. Her back hit the wall as he caged her without using his hands. Their lips brushed, and she sucked in his air, the full body of his flavour rolling over her tongue like a fine wine. He kissed her tenderly, not the white-hot passion she'd replayed over and over in her mind from the bar scene, but a worshipful caress that started and finished with their lips.

When he pulled away his pupils were huge, his smile even wider.

"Good night, Beth."

And he walked away, down the path that led into the trees.

Chapter Four

Daniel took his time making his way home, stopping by the swimming hole to stare into the swirling water. His thinking place—the spot he'd retreated to when the noise and bustle of being a part of huge family grew too much.

He'd needed to find quiet. The middle child of six, his daddy would joke, which meant he'd always had one or another of his brothers around. He'd learned to be the peacemaker, to walk the most serene path possible. At least in the public eye.

A ripple spread from the rock he tossed, small waves carrying across the slow-moving section of creek. Beth was a widow—he hadn't expected that. Something in her actions in the bar had struck him hard, and he wanted so badly to explore the way she had let him take control of her in that hallway before the time and place had ripped them back to reality. She hadn't acted like a grieving widow. She'd said as much, but she must have been with the man for a number of years. Lance had to be at least eight.

Heck, the boys were another whole issue. Daniel loved kids, but they weren't what he was focusing on right now. It was the woman who fascinated him. Although, if he did get involved with Beth, she'd probably have all kinds of rules about not seeing the kids and keeping things secretive. He had a buddy in town who was dating a single mom, and he'd shared stories that reminded Daniel of having to crawl in the windows at two a.m. to avoid the wrath of his daddy for missing curfew.

He stood and dragged his fingers through his hair. *Ahh, shit.* The vision of Beth's eyes haunted him. Why in the hell couldn't he just walk away? Did he want to have to hide and balance dating and dealing with kids? The ache in his belly screamed far louder than the warning in his brain.

It wasn't about being totally in lust, although getting to continue the adventure they'd interrupted so long ago excited him a lot. No, it was something else altogether. Something drew him and damn if he could deny the need.

Baggage and all, he was determined to see where this thing between them could go.

He strode through trees, twilight enough to guide his path. Before he even hit the porch, he smelled his daddy's pipe, the aromatic tobacco lingering on the air. Daniel took the steps two at a time, dropping himself into one of the comfortable chairs on the deck.

"Beth and the boys get home okay?" Mike puffed his pipe then blew a long slow stream of smoke into the air.

Daniel shook his head. "You adopting more strays? They got home fine."

His father rocked his chair a few times, the rhythm of the porch boards creaking soft and low. "She was surprised to see you today. You want to share what that's about?"

Daniel coughed. Last thing he wanted was to tell the truth. "No." His father raised a brow. "Sir."

Mike didn't say a word, just lifted his pipe to his lips. He smoked in silence, and Daniel tapped his fingers against his leg.

Damn it. His father did it to him every blessed time.

"I met her in Calgary when we took in a shipment of furniture in July. I hoped to see her again, but we...lost touch."

Silence reigned. The fall noises were subtler than the spring. The crickets fell silent earlier as the temperature dropped quicker in the evening. The soft sounds of the animals in the coop and the barns carried on the air occasionally, but it was a calm night. Peace filled his soul, the motions of his father rocking, even and slow, like a familiar balm. In the distance, the sound of the guest cabin door closing rang out.

"That'll be Blake saying good night to Jaxi. He'll be here soon." Mike pointed the mouthpiece of his pipe at Daniel. "I don't know it all, but that lady in the Peter's house needs some caring for." Daniel moved to speak but his father held up a hand. "If you're interested in her, you treat her nice. Understand, son?"

"I always treat ladies nice."

The firm command in his father's eyes made him hesitate. It was outrageous how he could be in his midtwenties and still reduced to a schoolchild by the man.

Blake wandered around the corner, his expression so dreamy Daniel couldn't hold in his chuckle. His father joined in and Blake grinned sheepishly.

"I look like a love-struck fool, don't I?"

The three of them laughed together, sitting on the porch in the full dark, and Daniel relaxed into the peace offered by his family. Finding Beth had turned all his previous plans to dust. Which was just fine—tomorrow was another day.

He could hardly wait.

Beth wandered the house after the boys finally settled. She wished it was as easy for her to put aside the excitement of the day and fade into sleep. The water boiled, and she made a cup of tea and carried it onto the porch to sip while she stared into the dark September sky.

Tell the truth, Beth. She sighed into her cup. Yeah, what she really wished for was someone to tuck her into bed.

And not just any someone—Daniel.

There was a part inside her that was scared to death of getting involved with a man again, but as her sister and parents had pointed out, not all men were like Samuel. Not everyone had the desire to control every facet of her life until she couldn't breathe.

But her late husband hadn't started that way either.

The next days passed in the usual blur of activity, getting the boys to the bus on time and rushing to her own teaching position. Arranging play dates and settling further into the community. She saw the Coleman boys around town occasionally, once Travis and once Blake, and both times her mind shot back to Daniel. No matter how full she made her to-do list, the damn man preoccupied her mind. After asking a few casual questions of her co-workers and other people she'd gotten to know, Daniel had come through with a squeaky-clean report.

Would getting involved with him really be so terrible?

By Friday, after a week's worth of crappy sleep where she tossed and turned all night, she'd come to a conclusion. She could wear out the battery-operated boyfriend she'd finally had the courage to purchase, or she could find another way to deal with the lust driving her. She didn't need a man in her life full time, but she sure could use one part time.

He'd offered. He was attracted to her. Maybe he'd even be willing to show her something other than sex in the missionary position.

As long as she was the one who got to call the shots, this

could work out well for them both.

The house was quiet, the boys all off at a birthday party. She stared at her reflection in the mirror, tucking her T-shirt in a little more, buttoning and unbuttoning her sweater. It was one thing to decide she was ready for some casual sex, another to inform Daniel of his role in that decision. Beth plopped down on her bed and sighed, her reflection taunting her. Yeah, the sleepless nights really added to her appeal as a sex symbol, dark shadows under her eyes. It took a rush of sheer willpower to force herself out the door and across the small bridge before she could change her mind, again. She'd never know if she didn't take the chance.

The barns and outbuildings on the other side of the trees were brightly lit, and she hesitated. She wasn't sure if she'd even find him at home on a Friday night, but there was no way she was going to phone. If nothing else, she'd walk to the main ranch house, say hello to Marion and Mike then retreat to the Peter's house to wait until it was time to pick up the kids.

She found him in the barn. Her throat and mouth flashed dry as she watched him rake something straw-like from a stall. The sleeves of his shirt were rolled up, and his biceps rocked with every pull of his arms. Tight muscles showed under the jeans, under his shirt—damn, he was just so good looking from boots all the way up to his slightly mussed hair. A throb hit between her legs and she bit her lip. There was nothing wrong with her physical response.

She took a deep breath. "Hey."

The delight in his eyes stirred more fluttering in her belly. "Beth. I didn't expect to see you here."

She glanced around. None of the rest of the Colemans seemed to be near. "You got a minute? My boys are at a birthday party and I..." Holy cow, this was harder than she thought it would be. She forced her head up and met his gaze. "We need to talk."

Daniel grinned, a panty-twisting expression that made her knees weak. He propped his rake against the wooden wall and tilted his head toward the door. "Come, we can talk while we walk."

"No." Her fingers were tangled together, and she dragged them apart, not sure where to put her hands. She felt about twelve years old with a first crush. "We're private here—that would be better."

He gestured to a bale. "Have a seat."

She'd practiced this so it didn't sound too desperate or sluttish. She hoped. "I was thinking about what you said the other day—"

"About us seeing each other?"

He sat beside her, their thighs touching as he faced the opposite direction. The scent of his skin rolled over her, the earthy fragrance of a man who'd done physical labour—raw and powerful. She barely stopped herself from leaning into him and offering her lips.

Instead, she nodded.

Daniel chuckled. "You're getting all tongue-tied again, Miss Beth."

"I'm interested in you, but I'm not looking for a long-term relationship." The words burst out exactly how she'd rehearsed them. She twisted to face him, determined to finish. "I think we should just have some fun together."

There. She'd said it. Maintaining eye contact was impossible, and she stared down at her fingers twisted together in her lap. He covered her hands with his, pulling one free.

"Now why did I think you were going to go and say

51

something like that?"

He did? "I mean, you're very attractive, but I don't think I should get involved with anyone. It's too soon and I don't want—"

"The boys, right?"

Exactly. She relaxed a little. "I don't think it's fair for them to see me with another man." Oh Lord, he was kissing her knuckles, his tongue teasing the seam between her fingers. The pulse between her legs quickened, and she had to force herself to stay motionless.

"Hmm. Makes sense, I guess." He opened her palm and kissed it. "So, you're interested in me sexually, but we can't see each other in public. Is that what you're saying?"

A shiver raced up her arm as he licked her wrist then gently sucked her skin.

"Yes. No. I mean..." How was she supposed to think with him touching her? When he leaned closer and nibbled on her earlobe? "Daniel, please."

"I aim to." He smoothed a hand over her shoulder, tangling his fingers in her hair. He pulled her head back so they could see into each other's eyes. "You want to spend time with me."

"Yes."

"But the boys can't know?"

She swallowed, watching his lips move closer. "Right."

"Hmm." He kissed her, lips faintly brushing back and forth as he directed the speed, the pressure. She slipped out her tongue to touch his bottom lip, and he captured her, sucking her tongue into his mouth. The kiss deepened, and she wrapped her arms around him, pressing as close as she could while seated side by side. The desire and need that had haunted her since the start of summer built to a high boil, and she gasped for air when he broke contact.

He traced a path over her body with his gaze. "How are we supposed to see each other without the little tykes catching on? And if they did find out, wouldn't that cause more trouble?"

No. No more thinking about it. She didn't want to analyse this anymore. She'd already had five restless nights trying to figure out how to satisfy her craving for him. "They won't know. We'll keep it quiet."

He reached for her chin. "So what you're saying, and pardon my crudeness, is you want a fuck buddy."

She cringed. The phrase had skipped through her brain earlier, but it sounded far worse when said out loud.

Daniel stroked his thumb over her cheek. "You're not looking for a friend with benefits because I ain't allowed to be your friend."

"It's not that, it's just—"

"Don't know if I can do that." She squeaked as he picked her up and placed her on his lap. "If all you're looking for is some sex, I'm not interested. There's a part of me that says, *hell yeah*, and I could be fucking you up against the wall in two minutes flat."

Oh God, the images racing through her mind.

"But if you remember our conversation in the back hall of the bar, I don't think you're that type of woman. I'm not that kind of man. Honesty is one of the things that makes us who we are, and I'm going to be honest with you, darling."

Beth held her breath as he cupped her face then stroked his other hand down her body intimately. He opened her legs and settled his fingers over her crotch. Could he feel how hot she was through her jeans?

"I find you very attractive, and I don't just mean your body.

I don't know what troubles you've had in your past, but I hope we'll get to talk them through at some point. So here's what I suggest—you tell me if you agree. You and I do both. We fool around like you want, as long as you let us try to learn to be friends, like I want."

It sounded so reasonable. Then he pressed a finger to the seam of her jeans and rubbed, and all logical thought fled. The slight friction against her clit was enough to cause an instantaneous reaction. She trembled in his arms. "I can't..."

He hummed, caressing the tender skin behind her ear, tracing patterns down her neck with his tongue. "I think you can do a lot of things, Miss Beth, if you put your mind to it."

The constant motion of his hand was driving her wild. "Please..."

Kisses descended again, and for the first time in a long time Beth let go. All her tension and fear she let fall away and simply accepted the rising passion. He was a thorough kisser, tasting her lips, her cheeks, brushing his fingers through her short hair and tugging her closer so their bodies melted together.

His hand moved relentlessly, and Beth widened her legs, rocking into his touch harder, needing a little nudge to push her over the edge. He slid his other hand under her sweater and cupped her breast through her T-shirt and bra, pinching her nipple. She teetered off the cliff, her sex pulsing with her orgasm as she moaned into his mouth. The physical bliss was so much richer than when she brought herself to a climax, and she closed her eyes to enjoy the sensations rocking her body.

It had been a very long time since a man had touched her like that.

When he finally separated them, her whole body buzzed. His grey eyes were dark, his pupils huge as he stared. Stared at her lips, her hair, her body. "You're beautiful when you come."

Beth glanced around the barn then laughed. "What am I doing?"

Daniel lifted her chin, and those fathomless eyes mesmerized her again. "You're dealing with the passion you've locked inside, for whatever reason." He didn't let her look away. "You on the Pill?"

Oh dear, this part of the conversation. She'd thought this through as well, but it was still tough to say. "I'm protected, but I want to use condoms."

Daniel shook his head. "We'll use them until we get a clean bill of health to show each other. If this is supposed to be fun for us both, condoms won't cut it for the long run. There are too many things I want to do with you. Plus, I want you to know I'm clean and not going to hurt you in any way."

Beth opened her mouth to protest then closed it. It made sense, even if the thought of anyone finding out he'd had blood work done scared her. She didn't want the whole town talking, but if they kept it quiet, she could make that change to her plans. "I'll get a test done when I go to Calgary at Thanksgiving. I have to see my doctor then anyway about my leg."

He touched the brace lightly. "Anything I need to be warned about? Any positions we need to be careful with while we're playing?"

"As if I would know," she answered without thinking.

"Beth?"

She flushed hard at his expression—the half-savage lust-driven animal, half-confused human thinker. He kissed her temple then lowered her back to the bale before rising and pacing a few steps.

"I need a few more details before we continue this adventure. You haven't had sex since your accident? Is that what you're saying?"

She hesitated. *Take control, Beth. Tell him what you want. Stay in charge.* "I haven't had sex, but I also..." The words stuck in her throat.

"You have three sons. I didn't imagine you were a blushing virgin."

What was it he had said? Be honest?

She lifted her chin and spoke as boldly as she could. "I've had sex on my back for ten years with one man. I want to do something different. I want to..." The conversation got harder and harder to continue. "I want to try it all."

He stopped in mid-pace, rotating slowly to face her. "What if your 'try it all' and mine veer apart?"

Oh dear.

Daniel continued, his voice gone husky and deep. "How about you make a list. Sound alright?"

She nodded, unable to force out any more words. Had she actually agreed to make a wish list of sexual positions and experiences?

Daniel held out his hand. "Come, I'll walk you home."

She glanced at her watch and swore. "I need to pick up the boys soon."

"I'm just walking you home, not ravishing you." He kissed her knuckles. "Not yet."

Beth swallowed hard. Holy cow. What had she done?

Chapter Five

Gabe Coleman stared his cousin down. Daniel tore his gaze from the chessboard for long enough to flash him the finger.

"Ha, getting pissy won't help you. Either you have the moves to make or you don't," Gabe taunted. One mistake later, Daniel groaned as Gabe slid his bishop across the board and took out the castle guarding Daniel's king. "Checkmate. Again," he gloated.

"Dammit, you never win this often."

"You don't usually suck this bad. What kind of mind-altering drugs you taking to be so brainless?"

Daniel eased back in his chair and grabbed his beer. "Nothing illegal or immoral. At least, not yet, anyway..."

Now that was interesting, coming from the most puritan of the Six Pack clan. Gabe popped up and headed for the kitchen. "Let me grab a refill, then I want details about that comment."

Their regular chess nights were far from regular, but Gabe always enjoyed the times he got together with his cousin. He tugged open the fridge and grabbed another couple of brews.

"Nothing really to tell. Nothing I would share. Maybe never anything." Daniel ended with a growl of frustration. He accepted the bottle Gabe held out then paced the distance between Gabe's tiny living room and the window overlooking the road.

While it wasn't anything near big enough to host a party,

Gabe found his one-bedroom apartment over the garage was a godsend—mostly because it had gotten him out from under his dad's roof.

"Sounds as if you've got a bee up your butt."

Daniel shook his head. "Just...you remember that woman the twins were teasing me about back in July? She's living in town."

"No shit. That's great."

"She's living next door to me in the Peter's house."

Fate had a twisted sense of humour. "Now, that's both great and weird."

"It gets weirder. She's sleeping in my old bedroom, and she says she's interested in me."

Gabe stopped in the middle of seating himself, caught in a half crouch. He laughed as he lowered himself the rest of the way to the couch. "You win. Totally the best story I've ever heard. Sounds like you've been a good boy and everything's coming your way for a change."

Daniel sighed. "Yeah, that was my response last Friday when she talked to me. But I've called her daily since, and every time there's been no answer."

"Screening her calls?"

"Maybe, or busy with her kids but—"

"Kids." Gabe raised a brow. "You didn't mention that to me last summer. About her having kids."

"I didn't know."

Silence hung between them for a minute. Gabe took a long swig of his beer as he calculated the best thing to say. Daniel deserved better luck in the female department than he'd gotten. "So...you think she's changed her mind?"

Daniel resumed pacing. "I don't know. I guess, I don't want

to push her, but dammit, she *said* she was interested."

"Exactly. So you should go after her. Seize the day, carpe diem, all that shit." Daniel made a rude noise and Gabe grinned. "Suck it up, that's what you're always throwing at me."

"And look how well it works. You're doing all the same old things you did before I started taunting you. Still sitting here, in what you called a piss-poor situation. Still not trying anything new. I mean, you came back to Rocky because you said it's what you want, but I don't see much cheering happening. Well, other than about your shiny new truck. But even that doesn't seem to be making you happy."

"Shiny it is, but you know it's more the bank's truck than my own. I'm making payments—I ain't dancing in the pot of gold at the end of the rainbow yet." They both sat heavily, bottles in their hands ignored. Gabe snorted in disgust. "We're damn sad creatures, ain't we? Twenty-nine and twenty—what are you again, twenty-five?"

"Six."

"Twenty-six, and stuck the same place we were last year. Except for you trying to trade up on girlfriends."

Daniel hissed. "Please, let's not bring Sierra into this. That's over and done, and if I never see her again, I'd be happy."

Gabe didn't blame him one bit. "Nothing worse than a woman deciding what you got isn't enough."

The music in the background thumped for a bit, then Daniel tossed back the rest of his drink and slammed the bottle on the tabletop. "You're right. It's time to take my own medicine. Carpe diem means now, and not down the road. And you're going to join me."

What the hell? "You tossed a few too many idioms into that last one, cuz, between medicine, fish and roads. What're we doing?"

"I'm going after a certain woman and getting a straight answer out of her. You...well, you're going to figure out the one thing you most need to do, and you're damn well going to do it."

The crazy enthusiasm shining in Daniel's eyes was contagious enough to get anyone's blood pumping. "One thing?"

"One thing. I mean, neither of us can make all the changes we want in one day, but we need to get started sometime, right?"

No shit. "So, is this a support group for procrastinators anonymous?"

"Damn right. You in?"

"Hell, yeah." Which one thing wasn't going to be easy to decide, but he could do it. "But I've got to think on it more before picking what to aim at."

Daniel moved back to the chessboard. "Hey, my task's easy. I get to track down a certain schoolteacher and convince her she will be seeing more of me. And that's while working around her teaching schedule, her kids and my chores."

"That's all. Sure sounds like a fucking spring breeze."

Daniel grinned. "Actually, you know what? I'm excited about the challenge of figuring her out and making her take me on. I mean, it ain't what I thought I'd be doing this fall, but it feels right."

Gabe thought hard. Yeah, there was no getting around that there wasn't going to be an easy thing to make some changes in his life, but it was damn-well time. "Excited isn't the first word that comes to mind, you know."

"Stupid, excited—same thing."

They moved back to the chessboard and began a new game, but this time Gabe found it tough to concentrate.

One step. The first step to changing things and making his

life better. What was it going to be? A million questions and ideas raced through his brain, all clamouring for attention.

Carpe diem. Seize the day. Maybe it *was* about time to do something other than simply drift.

Daniel leaned on the wall opposite her second-floor classroom, acknowledging the few students already dismissed from their classes. Two teenage girls giggled as they passed, eyeing him carefully, and he fought to hide his smile. He was far more interested in the woman waiting for him behind that door.

Even if she didn't know he was here yet.

After he'd dropped her back at the house on Friday and left her without a kiss, he knew she'd been confused. And still aroused, even after her climax. He'd wandered back into the trees, wishing he could jerk off like some horny teenager. He had a stupid desire to remain by the house and stare at her silhouette as she moved around the house—the urge was far too Peeping Tom-esque to be obeyed, but damn if he hadn't felt it.

Especially when a light flashed on upstairs right before the house slipped out of sight. Discovering she'd taken the room he usually slept in? He could picture in his mind what she saw around her, and the thought of being in the king-sized bed with her made his cock ache even harder.

Like he'd complained to Gabe, all he'd gotten was the damn answering machine, and now that it was Friday, time was up. If she'd changed her mind about wanting to see him, he wanted to hear it from her in person. Otherwise, enough of this pussyfooting around—she'd asked him for some experiences and he was dying to give them to her.

61

The bell rang, and he uncrossed his arms, shifting his weight forward as the door swung inward and a long line of students flooded out, laughter and chattering filling the air as after-school excitement rolled through the student body.

"Daniel."

He acknowledged one of the local boys they hired on a part-time basis to help around the ranch.

"You here to see Ms. Danube?" The youth grinned when he nodded, and turned around to shout back into the room. "Hey, Ms. D, you got a hot date or something?"

Daniel gave the kid a thump on the head with his knuckles. "Be polite, or you're mucking stalls all day long tomorrow." He eased past the rest of the bodies exiting and stepped to the side of the door, searching for Beth.

She stood behind her desk, frozen into immobility as she stared back. The room quieted, and she shook herself, turning away to stuff papers into a folder. She kept her eyes averted. "Daniel. I'm sorry, I wasn't expecting you."

"If you answered your phone, it wouldn't be a surprise."

She laughed, a snuffily sound that made the hairs on the back of his neck stand up. While she probably wouldn't appreciate being told it, she was kinda cute when she was embarrassed.

Her upper body shifted as she took a deep breath before turning to face him. "I'm just not sure how this is going to work."

"You changed your mind?" He spoke quietly, pulling the door shut behind him. She shook her head, and he let his satisfaction show in his grin. "Then we need to find a way to make it happen. Avoiding me isn't going to do the trick."

Her gaze flicked past him to the door. "You're not planning

anything here, are you?"

Oh damn. He hadn't, but her expression made him change his mind. "You thinking about dirty things to do in a classroom, are you now?"

"Daniel—we can't get caught."

Oh yeah, she definitely had something on her mind he hadn't expected. He paced back to the door and locked it, pulling down the blind to cover the only window into the room on the hall side. Second-story windows on the opposite wall? There was no way anyone could see in from that direction. He pivoted slowly on one heel to see she had the desk clutched so hard with both hands her knuckles were turning white.

"Boys' bus gets home at four thirty, right?"

She nodded.

He stepped closer, his cock slowly rising to press against the zipper of his jeans. She watched him warily, a mix of anticipation and anxiety in her eyes. "What I'd like to do is strip your clothes off, lay you flat out on the surface of your desk and fuck you senseless."

"*Jesus*, Daniel." The words escaped in a whisper, her eyes huge.

He dropped a hand over his cock and rubbed, attempting to get the damn thing to stop aching so hard. He swore he heard blood thumping in the back of his brain.

"You enjoy dirty talk, don't you?"

She breathed rapidly as he approached, the pulse in her neck drawing him like a magnet. "It makes me feel weak."

He lifted her and sat her on the desk, spreading her knees carefully, the heavy brace surrounding her leg clunking on the wooden surface. He hated to see the contraption on her, a constant reminder of the pain she must have experienced. Must still experience. One step took him between her thighs, and the warmth of their bodies connected. She gave a little moan, and his dick jumped involuntarily. Fuck, this was going to kill him.

"You made me a list yet?"

"I...I started to. It's at home."

He lifted her chin and licked her lower lip. Sweetness flooded his system. Damn she tasted good. He nibbled on the pouting flesh and stole one swipe into her mouth with his tongue.

She shivered.

He leaned away enough to stare into her eyes. "You keep the list. If I do anything you don't feel comfortable with, you just say no, and I'll stop."

"You don't want to read it?" The tension in her torso decreased a notch, and he smiled. They were now in full-body contact, and she was relaxed against him, all warm and soft, her breasts nudging his chest.

"I don't need to. If I miss anything you really want to try, I hope you'll tell me in person." He brushed their lips together, needing to taste her. Now that he knew where they'd end up, although not the when, he could enjoy and take his time.

She was a woman meant to be savoured, not gobbled in a rush.

If her heart beat any faster, she was going to fall over in a faint. The whole long masculine length of him pinned her in place, one hand on either side of her thighs as he leaned his torso against hers. The kiss he pressed to her lips was gentle, his tongue and lips moving over her like a placid breeze. She let herself stroke his chest, palms to the soft cotton of his shirt, the firm muscle underneath tempting her.

She checked her anxiety level. Nothing but a buzz of sexual desire ran through her veins, and she was so relieved. Beth drank in the sensation of power and passion mixing together in his touch.

Oh man, she was really going to do this. She wanted to. Needed to. It was another step in taking back control of her life. The life that had changed so subtly over the years she was still shocked she'd missed the signs of things going wrong. Her husband had made her feel incompetent and undesirable. The emotions Daniel raised were completely different.

He held her in place, his hips rocking slowly, the ridge of his cock branding her body as he dipped his tongue into the tender part of her ear. A shiver took her and he chuckled. "Miss Beth, you are making it very difficult to go slow."

She didn't want slow, not if fast meant she'd get to touch him sooner. She grasped his collar and pulled his lips back to hers, driving her tongue into his mouth and groaning as he rocked over her clit again.

They feasted on each other and time slipped away. Beth grew lightheaded, her limbs heavy. Blood pooled in her breasts, her sex, bringing with it an aching tingle of need. She wanted so much right now.

Daniel broke away and they both gasped for air. His eyes twinkled with mischief. "Sweet Lord, you're making me drunk on kisses alone." He held her cheek for a moment, brushing a thumb over her lower lip. "Hold still."

One button at a time he slipped her blouse open, their hips in contact as he opened the fabric to reveal her skin, her bra. Her breasts showed through the thin fabric, nipples puckered tight.

"That a favourite?" He ran a finger along the edge of the lace. Lord, he must be able to feel her heart pounding.

"No. Why?" He kissed her cheek again, a brief chaste kiss before pulling away, reaching for something on her desk. When he held up a pair of scissors her throat went dry. "What...?"

"Trust me?"

She fought the tremor of terror inside. She was in a classroom, for heaven's sake. He was a well-known and reputable man around town. Imagines of knife-wielding maniacs had no place in this fantasy.

"Yes," she squeaked.

"I'll buy you a new one." He pulled the fabric from her body and slipped his hand between the elastic and her skin. Then he put the tip of the scissor against his fingers and snipped. Deliberately, carefully, he cut away the supporting fabric of the cup, leaving behind the bones of her bra. The swells of her breasts were completely bare, the underwires remaining for support. He put the scissors away, slowly closed the drawer and piled the shreds of fabric on the edge of her desk. Every one of his movements made her expectations rise by the second.

Then he sat in her chair, adjusted the height and rolled between her legs. He kissed her belly button before looking into her eyes with that dark, dangerous expression she was coming to recognize and anticipate. It stole her breath away. Leaning forward, he licked a line up her torso, tonguing the fabric under her right breast. Another lap took him higher, drawing a circle around the tingling peak of her nipple. He sucked the whole tip into his mouth, pulsing his lips, and a line of heat drove from his mouth through her body straight to her core.

Oh Lord, it felt good. Every suck, every brush of his teeth on her skin made her feel more and more alive. From one side to the other he alternated, the cool air of the room brushing the wet skin he left behind, contrasting hard with the heat of his mouth. One hand, then two, came into play, cupping and lifting, massaging and pinching until she bit her lip to keep from crying out.

"You're beautiful, Beth, curvy and womanly in all the right ways." Another nip to the tender undercurve made her gasp, her panties soaked with the moisture flooding from her sex.

"Damn..." He suckled hard and stars formed before her eyes. "Daniel, please..."

She wasn't sure what she was asking for, only that she needed. Needed something more than what he was currently giving her.

He rose from the chair and caught the back of her head in one hand, drawing their mouths together while he played and teased her body with the other. Her muscles felt tight, ready to explode, and she rubbed wantonly against him, trying to find the missing component that nagged her.

Then he pulled away.

He stepped back, breathing heavily, and his gaze swept her body like a heated brand. He wiped his mouth carefully, then lowered a hand and adjusted himself through his jeans. A wave of desire rolled over her. Fucking on the desk sounded better and better by the minute.

They stared at each other, Beth clutching the edge of her desktop. The solid surface prickled her fingertips, the minute scratches from a thousand pens itching her hypersensitive skin.

Daniel stepped closer and tugged her blouse together, slowly doing up the buttons. The cool fabric brushed her nipples, driving her crazy.

"You have to pick up anything on the way home?" He smoothed his palms down her waist before lifting her off the desktop.

What? "Daniel, I..." Her nipples stood proud, stabbing the front of her blouse. "Aren't we going to do anything else?"

He chuckled as he touched a fingertip to one of the points. "I came to talk to you, to plan a date. You've got enough time to beat the boys home if we head out now."

The boys. Her blood was boiling, and she was going to die if she didn't get...something. But he was right.

"I can't believe you're stopping." Samuel would never have left himself unsatisfied.

"We've got time, sweetheart, and anticipation is a part of the fun. If you've had nothing but slam-bam sex, you may not know it, but delayed gratification is very rewarding."

She shook her head in frustration and turned to gather her things. "Didn't have it on the list you made me start, that's for sure."

He brushed the tattered bra scraps on her desk into his fingers then shoved them all into his pocket before offering her his hand. She accepted it, his clasp warm and solid. The admiration in his eyes felt good, even as the fabric rubbing her nipples sent shivers down her spine and made her sex ache. He unlocked and opened the door and offered his elbow.

"You really surprise me, Daniel." He made her body tingle, and not knowing what he was going to do next had the potential to drive her nuts. But it was a good uncertainty. She didn't feel as if he was a moment away from taking a swing at her, more of a "what's inside the box" kind of curiosity. She adjusted her jacket to cover her breasts better since her nipples still stood at attention.

"I surprise you because I think your body is beautiful?"

She stumbled, and he caught her, steadying her easily. The mischievous twinkle in his eye made heat flash across her face.

"Shh, not in the school." The second-floor hallway was

empty now, doors wide open, her fellow teachers gone already, but the echoes of voices grew louder as the two of them moved toward the stairs.

"You planning on hiding from me some more, Miss Beth, or are you going to start answering my calls?"

Somehow she had to make this work. No matter how awkward, she wanted it. "I'll answer. It would be best to talk when the boys are gone to bed. Can you call later in the evening?"

"I could. I could also come over."

The way her whole body reacted she figured something had to give, and soon. But she would stay in control of the situation.

"I don't think that's wise."

He tugged her to a stop, turning her to face him. "I'm not going to do anything to upset the boys on purpose, but either you're serious about this or you're not. I'm not going to be led around like some dog for you to pet when you get the urge. Either you say no right now, and I'll bow out of your life, or you stop saying yes with your body and no with your actions."

Beth's heart pounded, her mouth gone dry from a momentarily rush of fear. But when he stood close, his hands gentle on her arms as he looked into her eyes, there was nothing there that said he wanted to control her.

He only wanted her to decide.

"What's it going to be? Do you want to go ahead? You think about it, and let me know, because while I'm a patient man, Beth, I won't let you yank my chain like this. I won't let you start one way and expect you to change later because that's not fair to either of us. It's all or nothing. So why don't we make it your call. You contact me if you want to go ahead any further."

She hadn't been fair, even if she had good reasons to

hesitate. "It's impossible to think straight with my bra in pieces in your pocket."

A reluctant grin shimmered to life. "I'm hoping when you call, you say yes. Then the next time I cut something off you, it'll be your panties."

Beth swallowed, the racing beat of her heart making her lightheaded. He was right. She needed to stop being wishy-washy about this. Although, when they did find a time and place to be truly alone, she wasn't sure her body was going to survive.

Chapter Six

In the middle of clearing away supper dishes, Beth looked longingly at the recliner in the living room. A simple flick would light the gas fireplace, and she could lean back and rest her head on the soft cushions. The incredible sexual tension Daniel had lit in her body after school refused to diminish. Combined with the sheer workload of being a single mom—she was beat. A chance to put up her feet, even for a few minutes, would be paradise.

A crash jerked her from her blissful daydream. Nathan gasped then complete silence reigned. At her feet the broken bowl from the evening pasta dish lay in pieces. A few leftover noodles clung to the shards, the rest scattered over the floor like miniature snakes.

"Shit." Lance turned from the fridge where he'd been putting away the milk.

"No swearing." She held out a hand to keep the boys in one spot. "Don't move, I don't want you to cut yourself on the glass."

She grabbed the dustbin from under the sink and dealt with the larger pieces. Lance got the broom, and by the time the mess was cleaned up, the lethargy that had crept over her was gone. Which was good, since even though it was the weekend, she still had papers to mark and a lesson she wanted to revise. The boys needed homework spelling words checked and...

A soft sniff interrupted her mental rambling. Nathan stood

to the side of the kitchen, eyes wide, his face white.

"Nathan? You okay? Did you get cut when the bowl fell?"

He shook his head rapidly, tucking his hands behind his back.

Oh God.

"Honey, it's okay. It was an accident." She held out her arms, and he moved towards her slowly, warily. *Damn bastard of a husband.* "Mommy's not mad at you. I bet the bowl was slippery from the butter on the edge. We've cleaned it all up." She wrapped her arms around him and held him close, the rapid pitter-patter of his heart as it pounded in fear making her crazy.

She should have known better. She should have been stronger and dealt with Samuel long before he began to be such a dangerous influence in his sons' lives. He'd been so damn demanding and easily irritated. As the years passed, they'd all learned to walk on eggshells around him.

Breaking something had been akin to murder in Samuel's book.

Lance glanced back from where he stood at the sink, his young face twisted into a grimace as he fought not to cry. When he turned and started washing the dishes, Beth's soul ached a little more. It was so like him—her firstborn—once again trying to act the grown up. Caring and acting beyond his years.

A sense of frustration swept her. What was she doing? There was so much she needed to deal with, repercussions from ten years of mental abuse. How was she supposed to be able to make things better for her boys when she felt instant fear when the situation deviated even minutely from the "proper way"?

What she wouldn't give for a cup of coffee and a good long talk with a sympathetic ear to listen. She didn't want to talk to the school counsellor and bring the whole mess into her new workplace. She didn't want to return to the stony-faced therapist she'd been seeing in Calgary.

Daniel crossed her mind again and her face warmed. She stood, still cuddling Nathan, and shuffled her way into the living room. Her leg ached, but she wasn't about to put him down. He needed her. Heck, she needed him. They settled together in the big armchair. The grading could wait. The lesson—she'd put aside her usual method of getting all their work out of the way immediately and instead make time to check it over during the next couple of days.

Tonight her boys needed a reminder that life was not as confining as it used to be.

"Lance, honey, leave the dishes. I need your help here."

He joined her, sitting next to his little brother on the couch. Robbie clutched his security blanket in his hand, a defiant look in his eyes.

Her husband had hated that blanket.

"I think we're settled into the school year enough we need to start planning some fun activities to do together. You guys got any ideas? What would you like to do as a family?"

Nathan wiggled a bit, his face brightening. "You mean like going swimming or stuff?"

Beth groaned inside but hid it behind a smile. "Yes. Only I don't think you should use the swimming hole anymore this year, right? We'll go to the pool. Anything else?"

Together they made a list of suggestions, and the mood in the house lightened. Beth gave thanks the kids were resilient.

A couple of hours later, after multiple games of Snakes and Ladders, cups of hot chocolate—with marshmallows—and an endless number of slightly tuneless songs bellowed out during bath time, the three boys were finally all tucked into bed. A glance at the clock showed it was only nine p.m., but she could have sworn it was close to midnight. She was ready to crawl into her own bed and take the weight off her aching limb.

She really should get back to her to-do list and not give in to the temptation to soak for an hour then head to bed herself. And yet, why not? Abandoning all plans of productivity, including ignoring the dishes in the sink, didn't mean she was evil. There were two days stretching ahead on the weekend to get her stuff done.

Mom break, starting now.

She got the tub running before grabbing a glass of wine and her book. Soaking in the hot water made her feel halfway human again. It also gave her plenty of time to daydream about the sensations Daniel ignited in her body. Her book abandoned to the floor, she wondered where the line was between getting what she wanted physically and discovering what Daniel offered in addition to the sex.

Friendship.

She dried off and pulled on her thick pyjamas, all the while debating with herself. Daniel wanted an answer. She stared at the phone. *Damn it.* Without letting herself think it through anymore, she punched in his number and waited for a response.

She'd had enough years of being careful, and it was time to keep this ball rolling.

"Colemans'," a deep voice answered, and she hesitated. It kind of sounded like him but...

"Daniel?"

The man at the other end laughed. "You're close. Only five more guesses."

She smiled in spite of her nervousness. "Jesse."

"Now how did you do that?"

It was her turn to laugh. "Of all the boys, I figured you were the only one who'd play games on the phone."

"Yeah, well, don't tell my mama. Just a minute, I'll get him for you."

The echoing silence gave her time for the image of Jesse and Joel dancing with Darleen to pop back into her brain. What was it that Daniel had said? The boys...shared? The thought intrigued her. Not with them per say, but the whole two guys paying attention to her—about as far from the vanilla missionary sex forced on her over the years as she could imagine.

The temptation to add to her list was strong. Daniel said he didn't want to see it anymore, so why not? It would be one of those inspirational things—find a few books, read about it and get turned on. Reading about it was enough for now.

Actually, having more than one guy paying attention to her at one time was probably one of the better-imagined-than-done things. Wouldn't there be too many limbs and body parts touching and connecting? A sudden throb between her legs surprised her. Okay, lots of body parts touching *her* would be fine.

"Beth?"

How had she ever mistaken Jesse for Daniel? The deep timbre of his voice made her toes curl. It took a few seconds to drag her mind back to the reason why she had called. "Hey, you asked me to phone. I know it's late, but do you have a few minutes to talk?"

A pause. "Is this going to be a good talk or a bad talk?"

"I'm not calling it off." *There*, it had been said. "I need...I need some advice, beyond the...issue we're going to..."

He laughed. "You can't even say the word sex when you're on the phone. Damn, you are one hundred percent charming."

"And you're a tease."

"What kind of advice can I get for you tonight?" There was a creaking sound, and the voices in the background faded away. "I'm out on the porch and no one's listening. We can chat if you'd like. Or I can come over there."

Beth glanced at her watch. She was going to be bagged tomorrow. "I'm all ready for bed, and the boys are bound to be up at their usual time. Plus, I slacked off on all my work tonight putting out fires."

"Troubles?"

She sighed. "Kind of, but it was a good evening in the end. The kids and I made a list of things they want to do. Only some of them..."

He sat silently on the other end of the line, waiting for her to continue. When he chuckled, it was light enough to help calm her. "You're going to have to help me here with a few more details. I can't tell if that's a 'some of them require snow to fall', or 'some of them need you to have twelve hands' and you'd like my help."

For not wanting to get involved with him, the temptation to have him around grew by the minute. The boys liked him, by all reports he was a safe man to do things with.

Her body craved him.

She couldn't decide if that final reason held her in restraint or egged her on. "Daniel, can I back up about twelve paces and ask a real big favour of you?"

"What's up, darling?"

"They want to go swimming."

He whistled low. "Water's going to be fairly brisk this time of—"

"At the pool. But with my bad leg it's hard for me to play with them. Would you be willing to come with us sometime? I hate to disappoint them, and it might be a good way to, well, you know. Your part of our deal."

"Become friends?"

"Yeah." She stumbled down the stairs to turn off all the lights and make sure the door was locked. Leaving it unlatched—she couldn't believe she'd done that the other day. "There's an open swim both days of the weekend. The times are listed online. If either of them work for you."

"You want to go tomorrow?"

That easy, huh? "You don't have commitments already?"

His rich laugh spread over her like a balm. "I've always got stuff on the go, but that's the good part about friends—they make time for each other. I can take a couple of hours off to join you and the boys. The twins came home this weekend from college, so they can help out around the ranch. You want me to pick you up? The kids would love riding in the jump seat of my truck."

They would, but she didn't want to push this that fast. "I'll meet you there. Thanks, Daniel."

"Not at all. I get to see you in a swimsuit out of the deal as well, right?"

With one sentence, he stole her voice. She was going to see him in not much more than his briefs, and suddenly this wasn't sounding like a very safe public activity.

"Beth, you still there?"

"I'm..."

"You're blushing, aren't you? Is the thought of me looking you over making you tingle in certain spots?"

"Oh God, stop it."

He laughed again, and the tingles he'd mentioned spread. "You ever have phone sex, darling?"

He paused until she had to answer. "No."

"The boys in bed?"

"Yes."

"Hmm, then I think you have to give me a minute." The squeak of the porch door carried over the phone, and voices flickered in and out of the background. "I want to be able to join you."

"Join me?" *Phone sex. Holy cow.* Her panties were wet and getting wetter by the second.

"Beth, are you in your bedroom?"

"No," she squeezed out through a throat gone dry. Her heart pounded, and her clit thumped in time with her heart.

He sighed, a long relaxed sound. "That's better. I'm in my room. I want you to go to your room and lock the door so you're not worried about the boys interrupting you."

"Daniel, I..." Her feet moved up the stairs involuntarily, like puppet strings drew her forward. It was awkward, manoeuvring straight-legged with the brace on one side.

"You don't want to do this, you just tell me, but I think you'll enjoy it."

She swallowed hard. "I want to." Oh yeah, she really wanted to.

"Are you in your room?"

She turned the lock. "Yes." The whole space somehow looked different. Brighter, cozier. More sensual. The sound of his breathing on the other end of the line teased her. Heated her already steamy blood.

"Take off your clothes and crawl under the covers. It's cold in that big room this time of year. You got any toys handy?"

"Toys?" she squeaked.

"If I were there, I'd be touching you. Running my hands over your skin. Kissing your beautiful breasts. Stroking your pussy. If you got a vibrator or something, go grab it, just to help out a little, until I'm really there."

He was asking if she had a vibrator. A man who made her blood boil with a single glance was talking about sex toys. A shiver ran over her skin, and her breathing sped up. "I've...I've got to put the phone down." *Oh God, did she just admit to him she had one?*

"I'll be here when you pick up. I'm taking off my clothes as well. Thinking about you is getting me harder than a spike."

Beth lowered the phone to the bed, her hand shaking slightly. Phone sex? She hadn't been this turned-on in forever. The teasing anticipation begun by Daniel's touch at the school reactivated. She unlocked her side drawer and grabbed her vibrator. A laugh escaped her as she tossed it on the bed. She wasn't going to need much to go off, her body already tight and aroused from the sound of his voice. She sat and leaned over to undo the buckles that held her brace in place. The rush of relief from being out of its confines fled rapidly in light of other more distracting matters, and she let the contraption drop unminded to the floor. A couple of wiggles took care of her pyjamas and she dove under the thick quilt.

Suddenly she felt very lonely and a touch shy. Phone sex. *Sheesh.* If she weren't so excited, she'd think it was a little pathetic.

She took a deep breath to steady her nerves before picking up the phone. "Daniel?"

"Hmm, right here. You all cozy in that big bed? Your

nipples still tight from the cold of the room or you warming up already?"

A flash of electricity shot up her spine. "You just jump right in, don't you?"

"Are they tight?"

"Yes." Like rocks. And they ached for his mouth, for the pull of his lips she'd felt that afternoon.

"Touch them. Damn, I loved seeing you today. Sexy as sin with your tits showing through the fabric of your blouse, like they were playing peek-a-boo for me." He hummed, a deep vibrating noise that stroked her eardrums and melted something inside. "You tasted like pure pleasure. Rolling my tongue around your nipples and sucking on them made my cock ache. I want you to touch yourself. How do you want it? You like your breasts massaged? You enjoy what I did to you today?"

Beth had lain back against the pillows when he started talking, propping the phone by her ear. To hell with being embarrassed, this was hot. She cupped her breasts in her hands and squeezed and rubbed like he had earlier in the day. Slow tugs on her nipples as she imagined him sucking them.

"I liked it," she whispered, the words sultry and deep to her own ears.

"You like it hard? If I were to lean over you on the bed, press my weight on top of you and suck your nipple into my mouth hard, would that turn you on?" He paused, his breathing rough on the other end of the line. "Or you want me to play with you slowly? Tongue around your sweet red nipples again and again?"

"Tonight I want it hard." She pinched as she answered, the tingle in her groin growing as her breasts grew more sensitive.

"Shit, yeah, tugging and biting until you make those sexy

moaning sounds deep in your throat." He growled, low and husky. "You taste so good, your skin is hot against my lips. I'm going to touch your pussy the next time I see you. Slowly take my fingers and open you up to find out what pleases you."

She whimpered, wishing he were there, doing it right at that moment.

"Touch your clit, Beth, use your vibrator if you want, but imagine it's my mouth and my fingers down there. Licking and exploring, circling your sweet pussy and dipping inside."

She fingered and teased herself, flicking the vibrator on and following his voice, moaning as his directions brought her closer to climax by the second.

He panted in her ear. "I can imagine how you're going to taste and I can hardly wait. I'll push my tongue into you, deep inside, reaching for the sweet cream from your body. Circling your clit again." He swore softly. "God, Beth, I want to touch you so fucking badly right now. Want to fill you up. Put something into your pussy for me, so I can think about being the one to press in. Stretch yourself full."

The vibrator was cold and plastic, and she would have given anything at that moment to have him really there with her, his hot skin over hers, his breath warming her, the scent of sex in the air.

"What are you doing, Daniel? While you're talking to me? Are you...hard?" Her inhibitions melted away with the heat of desire rippling through her.

"Hard? Hell, I've got my fist around my cock and it's not enough. I can't wait to have your mouth on me. To see your lips surround me and have you suck me." Beth let out a moan, wondering what it would feel like to touch him that intimately. To hold him in her mouth and taste his seed. "I imagine your tongue touching me, and my balls ache. I want more than your mouth—I want to fuck you hard. Slip the head of my cock against your sweet pussy and drive in like a hammer."

She groaned, the wicked words making her hotter than she'd ever expected. She pressed her vibrator against her clit. "Where are we?" Her voice sounded hollow, her ears full of the rush of blood pumping through her veins.

"I've got you bent over the seat of my truck, your ass bare, your pussy all wet and ready for me." The soft echo of a slapping sound carried over the line. Oh my God, that was him, stroking himself in the background. The knowledge was so carnal and raw, she could barely stand it. "I get to watch every second of fucking you this way, your pussy lips hot and swollen around my cock."

From behind. Beth flipped her mental imagine and rubbed her clit harder, plunging the warm plastic into her needy core.

"Your ass looks so good, I'm tempted to take my cock and squeeze my way in there, let you—"

"My ass?" she gasped. The tingling grew harder and hotter than before. Anal sex had never been on the agenda. Until now.

"You like that idea, do you?"

She couldn't even breathe.

"Not this time, darling, I'm getting too close. I want to feel you come around me. Squeeze my dick when it's buried deep in your body. I'm gonna fuck you hard until you can't stand it anymore, my fingers on your clit, my cock—"

"Daniel, *ohhh...*" She came, the waves fast and hard, shaking her body and making her gasp in pleasure.

"Yeah, do it. Fuck, I can't..." He groaned in her ear and another delicious pulse struck. She let it take her, the vibrator slipping from her body, her touch on her clit slowing as her sensitivity rose. The blood pounding in her ears deafened her for a second, her climax rolling slowly down as she pictured him bent over her, still buried inside. As trite as it was, she figured that was as close to the earth moving as she'd ever gotten. They both lay speechless for a moment, the echo of their harsh breathing the only sound carrying over the receiver.

"Holy hell, woman, I can't wait until I'm really with you."

She laughed, revelling in the sense of freedom washing over her. "I feel about sixteen years old. Except I'd never dreamed of phone sex at that age."

"I'm damn glad you're not sixteen. Shit, I'm getting hard again, just thinking about what you must look like right now. I bet your skin is flushed and warm, and you're all soft and cuddly."

Boneless was a better word for it. It took actual effort to answer him. "You like cuddling, Daniel?"

He hummed, soft and low, and a trace of a shiver flitted over her skin. Damn, he turned her on.

"I like sex, and cuddling is a part of it. I love how cuddling slips into sex."

"Really?" She rolled over, slipping the vibrator into the drawer with her last burst of energy. She'd wash it when she woke. Right now, sleep beckoned.

"Hmm, really. I'm going to take you in the morning sometime, when you're all soft and drowsy. I'll slip into you and bring you to an orgasm as you wake."

"Stop it. You'll be getting me all worked up again."

He laughed. "You relaxed now? Feel better?"

"Hmm, yeah." Thinking about anything right now was virtually impossible. "See you tomorrow?"

"Can't wait. Sleep well."

Beth clicked off the phone and dropped it on the side table.

After turning off her light, she buried herself in the toasty quilt. The sexual euphoria in her body lulled her to sleep. Tomorrow would be soon enough to think things through.

Chapter Seven

Rafe stared open mouthed. "For serious?"

Gabe sighed. "I've been doing the math, and if we don't change something, we're not going to have enough land or animals to support even one of us, let alone you, me and the folks."

His kid brother paced to the nearest bale and sat with a plop. "Shit. I thought it might get tight, but nothing like that. What did Dad say—?"

"Ain't told him yet. I wanted to run something past you first."

Rafe's eyes widened, the vivid blue in them hitting hard, a warning beacon gone wrong. "You did up the books without letting Dad know what you found?"

"He doesn't know I was in them in the first place."

"Holy fuck. You're really looking for some trouble."

The phantom pain of getting back-handed halfway into tomorrow shook Gabe, but not hard enough to make him change his path. It wasn't only that Daniel had egged him on. Time to find one thing to change that would make a difference. This was the one thing, the right thing to do. Years too late, if he was honest. "If we want to have a place to live and call home down the road, and if Mom and Dad aren't going to end up begging for favours from the rest of the family, we need to start planning for changes now."

His brother nodded slowly, but his doubt remained clear. "You talk about having a place to call home. Seems to me not that long ago Rocky was the last place you wanted to be."

Gabe couldn't deny it. Couldn't deny the guilt he now felt at having left Rafe in a tough situation when not even in his teens. "I left. It's true, and you know why. But you have to admit I came back and I've worked damn hard since then. If there was a way to make those years I was gone easier on you, I should have done it. I was just so bent on getting away from the old man and his know-it-all ways, I didn't even think of you."

"Didn't expect you to." Rafe looked even younger than usual as he picked up a length of rope and started coiling it. "But that doesn't change the fact that Dad and you don't see eye to eye on a lot of things. You saying we need to make some big changes to the ranch is going to go over like a pile of manure. I don't want to get caught in the crossfire again."

They stared at each other for a minute before Gabe broke eye contact and paced away. "Understood. Which is why I wanted to talk to you before I said anything to Dad. So the first question is—do you want to keep going once you're done with school?"

"Ranching? If we can afford it, hell yeah."

Which was pretty much what Gabe had expected. "So the next question is, what part? You willing to give up...what, in order to keep doing the rest?"

Rafe shrugged. "I want to work outdoors. I want to work with the animals. If we could find some way to get rid of extra fields, I'd be good with that. But the animals are probably my top choice."

"That's what I thought. So I'm going to do some research into how we can make this ranch viable again. Enough to support three families, if possible. Once I've got the information in place, then we can talk to the folks. Because facts are facts, and it's tough to argue with solid figures and cold hard cash."

The rope, twisted off and neatly coiled was hung on the wall. Rafe moved on to the next piece of equipment, polishing and cleaning as they talked. "It sounds good, but you know facts mean shit to him at times."

Gabe eyed the faint white line of the scar running down Rafe's cheek. "We'll set any meetings up when he's stone-cold sober, and there's as much money in the bank as possible. Rafe, this ain't happening overnight. And the doom and gloom I'm seeing in the books isn't about to fall on us tomorrow. I'm just...thinking for down the road."

His brother laughed, his blond head tossed back even as his hands kept moving as he dealt with chores. "Now I wonder if you're the one who's been drinking. Talking about the future and planning for families. I thought you didn't want a family."

"I don't. I was talking about you. And Mom and Dad."

"Still don't know what your trouble is about having a family someday."

A flash of a smile and a soft hand brushing his cheek came back to haunt him. Gabe's gut twisted, and he shoved the memories to the farthest corner of his mind. "There's no family in my future. Be done with poking that question at me, okay? But that doesn't mean I want to be out on the street or having to work in some big-box store hawking video games or flipping burgers at a fast food joint. There's nothing like living here, and I don't want any of us to have to give it up, not even Dad. Because when he's not being a jackass, he's done his best over the years."

Rafe shrugged. "Fine. Do your research, and I'll keep my mouth shut. But don't be stupid and let it out early what you're up to. Do me and my bones a favour."

Gabe dropped an arm around his brother's shoulder and gave him a squeeze. "I'll be careful, and I'll make sure that what we got doesn't get lost. You can trust me."

Another bit of gear resumed its position on the wall, and Rafe brushed his hands off with a grin. "So, now that you're in the big-brother-talking-and-planning mode, what say you help me plot some ideas about how to get Jenna to give me a second look. Damn girl is being stubborn."

Oh Lord. Giving advice on romancing to his little brother. Just what he wanted. "Fine. Let's finish chores, and I'll find you a beer at my place. We can talk all about your lousy love life and I'll try not to laugh."

"Fuck you," Raphael spoke with no venom in his tone, winking to ease the sting.

They worked together easily, and Gabe smiled. Yeah, it was good to be heading down a new path, even if it wasn't going to be an easy route.

Daniel waited by the pool doors for Beth and the boys to arrive. This was their third meeting at the pool, and he was looking forward to today's swim.

Getting involved with Beth had pretty much worked out as he'd expected. Trying to find time to spend together with the boys around made life very difficult. Oh, the two of them had met for coffee, and he'd joined her picking up groceries. They'd even managed to "accidentally" meet while walking a few evenings. But none of these circumstances offered any real time alone, and there were only so many things they could safely talk about in public or around the kids. While he was fine with taking his time to romance the woman, they weren't going to ever get past this stage if he didn't do a little wrangling.

Luckily, wrangling was something he was damn good at.

Beth pulled up in her SUV. The boys poured out as soon as the lights dimmed and the engine turned off.

"Daniel! Come on, hurry, hurry." Excited beyond belief, the three of them had enough power to drag him off his feet without even trying.

"Hey, guys, let me help your mama for a minute, then we're good to go." Lance eyed him as he moved forward, offering a hand to Beth. The kid watched him like a hawk around Beth, and there was no way he wanted to be explaining anything to an eight-year-old when there still wasn't anything to explain.

"Morning, Daniel."

He loved how she blushed. "Morning. You ready for some fun in the water?" Oh hell, he hoped so.

She gave him a suspicious look. "Come on, boys. Let's not keep Daniel waiting."

Inside the doors the little guys scattered, pulling off their boots and bouncing outside the change-room door like grasshoppers. Beth laughed at them, a light and rested sound, and Daniel felt something inside turn over. The draw he felt toward her wasn't diminishing, and it wasn't only caused by sexual frustration.

"Sleep well?" he asked softly.

She flicked a glance his direction. "Like a baby."

They grinned at each other. He'd phoned last night and suggested he should come over. When she'd offered another excuse, he'd gotten them both off again, talking about surprising her with wild sex out behind the barn. He was getting damn good at talking dirty, but it was time for something other than climaxes in separate rooms. Separate houses.

Daniel had to adjust his stance to make room to take the pressure off his rising cock. Fuck, getting into a swimsuit was going to be dangerous.

Beth swiped the boys' pool passes. Daniel coughed to get her attention. He leaned toward to the attendant. "You still have room in the water-games program?"

She pulled a clipboard out and checked it. "Five slots available."

Beth frowned. "What's that about?"

The girl perked up. "Something new we're trying out. It's a drop-in program, and we've got instructors to supervise and lead the kids through all kinds of games and activities in the pool. There's no extra charge, and they get to try diving and water polo, and use the equipment. It's a lot of fun."

"Mommy, can we do that?" Bouncing bodies surrounded them, hands clutching at Beth, three sets of eyes pleading. Daniel smiled at her expression, her sheer delight at seeing the boys' enthusiasm.

"Of course you can. If you're old enough." Beth turned to the counter. "Eight, seven and six. Is that okay?"

The girl nodded. "Definitely." She held up wristbands, and three little arms shot out to get tagged. She gave instructions while she fastened them on. "You need to get changed, have a shower then join the group in the kiddie pool. That's where you're starting in..." she checked over her shoulder, "...ten minutes. But remember to walk on deck, right, guys?"

"Yes, ma'am!" Excitement carried in their voices.

Nathan tugged on Beth's arm. "Are you going to play with us too, Mommy?"

"I think it's only for big boys like you guys. I'll take it easy in the hot tub. Is that okay?"

He squirmed with excitement. "Daniel can play with you. That way you won't be lonely."

Yeah, that was exactly what Daniel had in mind. He glanced up to see Beth staring back as her sons tugged her awkwardly toward the change room, her face flushed.

Daniel winked before turning to double-check. "The program runs for an hour?"

The girl behind the counter shook her head. "An hour and a half. That okay?"

"That's just fine." *In fact, it was fucking marvellous.* He slipped his shoes off at the rack and made his way down the hallway to make sure the second part of his plan would work as well. Once the boys were happy and cared for, he and Beth were going to have a little alone time.

Chapter Eight

"You planned this, didn't you?"

"I did." Daniel put her crutches to the side and helped her down the stairs into the hot tub.

She took another glance around the pool area. Her boys were already having a blast, screaming and yelling and doing cannonballs with the group. Daniel slipped his hand off her shoulder and tugged on her waist, drawing her to his side. There were a few other moms sitting on the deck in the plastic chairs, noses buried in books or chatting quietly together. A few smiled her direction, but no one seemed to think anything of her and Daniel sitting intimately together in the hot tub.

"I saw the notice last week when we were here, and thought it might offer a solution to our problem."

His lips hovered over her ear, the hand at her waist rubbing the bare skin of her back. She didn't do bikinis, not after three kids in three years. She was glad that the mess on her leg didn't seem to bother him at all either. The scars from the car crash were beginning to fade from her leg. The scars on her heart? Maybe they were starting to go as well.

Fingers fleetingly brushed her thigh, and she took a quick breath.

"Our problem?"

"Getting alone."

Another stroke, higher this time. She shivered in spite of the heat of the pool. "Daniel, what are you doing?"

He leaned back, resting his head on the tiles. "Trying to decide what I'm going to do to you first." His dark grey eyes bore into her and she swallowed. Her libido kicked up a few notches.

"First? Here?" The words squeaked out of her. *Oh. My. God.* "Daniel, we're in public. We can't..." He grabbed her foot and tugged it into his lap, rubbing her insole hard with his thumbs. "That feels good." She adjusted her position until she sat across from him, propping her other foot on him without any hesitation.

He chuckled. "You mean I only needed to offer a massage all this time to get you into my evil clutches?"

She returned his grin and winked. "I'm easy that way." The instant heat that smouldered back made her sex ache. Beth closed her eyes and sank into the water, enjoying his touch far more than any massage she'd gotten since the accident.

The last couple of times they'd come to the pool, Daniel had been all about the kids. Oh, he'd been courteous and helped her get where she needed to go, but he'd kept most of his attention on the boys, enticing them to try a few floats and swimming strokes. Playing tag and generally wearing them out. She'd relaxed in the warm water of the kiddie pool, clapping and waving every time the request "Look at me, Mommy" echoed.

Something warm had sprouted in her heart as she watched him with her sons, seeing him without any agenda except to have fun and enjoy their company.

It gave her hope, far more than she wanted it to.

Now he turned all that focused attention on her. He rubbed and caressed her feet, one at a time, then switched back and did her calves. By that time she was boiling alive between the heat of the water and the heat of his touch. Her breasts ached, and the core of her body felt hollow and empty. When he tugged her by the hand, she shook herself alert, slightly dazed.

"Come on." Daniel helped her out of the hot tub, draping her towel around her neck before offering his elbow. She limped at his side, leaning on his arm for balance. He carried her crutches in his other hand, the ones she used to get around in the change room until she put the brace back on.

"Where are we going?"

"For some non-vanilla."

She stumbled and he steadied her quickly. "You're not serious," she hissed.

"Never been more serious in my life."

Holy cow, he was too.

He nodded politely at the ladies as they manoeuvred past the deck chairs. One woman eyed him hungrily, and Beth wanted to hang a sign around his neck saying *Taken.*

Where the hell had that come from? She beat down the feelings of jealousy as fast as she could. Daniel and her were...friends...although it appeared they were about to enjoy some benefits. *Sweet Jesus.* The heat racing over her skin had nothing to do with the hot tub they'd just left.

Daniel took the side hallway between the men's and ladies' change rooms, glancing behind them cautiously before opening a door and leading her in. It was one of the family change rooms. The rectangular room held a small wall-mounted bench and a larger shower enclosure at the far end. He leaned the crutches against the far wall then closed the door. The click of the lock echoed loud in the room.

"Daniel, what—?"

He spun her in his arms, and swallowed the question. He

took control of her lips, clutching their bodies together tightly, kissing her madly. She gave in, the need for him having built too high over the past days to try and deny anymore.

Teeth and tongues, wet touches, simmering need. All she could do was feel, all she could think about was the way her body reacted. He peeled off one shoulder strap of her tank-top suit and fastened his mouth to her breast. Sucking the tip hard, he nipped and licked and drove her mad. He leaned her back on the wall and peeled down the other strap, one hand cupping the round of her breast before feasting on it in turn. Every nerve in her body sang. The constant ache in her leg faded to nothing as pleasure rose higher and higher. She ran her fingers through his hair, holding his mouth to her intimately. The repetitive tug of his lips teased and ramped up her need.

It only took a second for him to strip away the rest of her suit, and her hands flew upward in an attempt to cover her torso.

"Darling, you're gorgeous. Don't hide, don't let yourself doubt how fucking incredible it makes me feel to see you naked in front of me." Daniel spoke quietly, his hands clasping her fingers gently and tugging her arms to the sides. Beth planted her palms against the wall for balance, her legs spread wide.

"Sweet mercy, woman." He drew a finger down her torso as he knelt at her feet, and her belly fluttered under his touch. He leaned closer and took a deep breath in through his nose. "I can smell your desire. You're wet just thinking about what we're going to do, aren't you?"

Her legs trembled. "What are we going to do?"

His wicked grin flashed. "I already told you. Non-vanilla. We've got forty-five minutes left."

With one hand he separated the curls of her body, touching

her slowly, his gaze never leaving hers. Again and again he circled a finger along the sensitive skin of her sex, her labia and her clit pulsing in time with her heart. A single finger slipped into her depths, and he licked her clit and she moaned.

"You can make some noise, but no screaming, okay? I'll take you somewhere for the screaming sex another time."

"Jesus, Daniel, shut up already and...hell." He bit her clit and the top of her head nearly blew off, it felt so damn good. Another finger joined the first, and he stroked and teased her, inside and out now, his tongue moving rapidly against her throbbing clit. His fingers plunged into her faster and faster until there was no hope of holding back, and her orgasm flashed like a wild fire. He slowed his strokes, drawing out the waves until she grasped his head and dragged him away from her now-too-sensitive center.

He rose, and those eyes caught her in his spell. He stripped off his swim trunks, and she swore at the size of him, his erection slamming into his belly as he stood. He pulled a condom from the towel on the counter, rolled it on and stepped closer.

"Daniel, how are we going to—?"

He kissed her wildly, that massive cock caught between their bodies, the heat of it branding her belly. When he finally pulled away, they both gasped for air.

"Fucking need to be inside you. Now."

"Yes, please...yes." She would have begged for longer but there was no need. Her desperation was reflected in his eyes as well. He stood her on her good leg and took hold of her injured one.

"Tell me if this hurts."

He lifted her thigh slowly, cautiously, watching her face the whole time. The angle took the pressure off the nerves that were usually pinched and sore, and she tugged his hips to get him closer to where she needed him. "It's good, it's good. Oh God, now, *please.*"

He lined up the head of his shaft, nudging against her labia, slowly opening her. He rocked his hips a few times, slipping against her, and it felt so amazing she panted for air, clutching him in an attempt to pull him farther in.

He clasped her chin with his free hand and, as their eyes met, powered into her body.

Full.

Stretched apart.

Aching and wanting and—damn, it felt amazing. She watched his eyes flicker for a second before he dropped his forehead to hers. "That is about the hottest sensation I've ever felt. Fuck." He took a deep breath. "You good, darling?"

There was no way on earth she could speak. She nodded.

Slow, even, tortuous, wonderful. He withdrew, paused, then thrust in again. Her breath shot out as his cock rocketed in, and she clutched his shoulders, closing her eyes to let the sensations take control. Let him take control.

He filled her completely, his girth stretching her more than she ever remembered. Maybe it was the angle, maybe it was because they were both panting with desire. Maybe it was the fact that outside the door there were people innocently swimming laps, but she'd never been so turned on before in her life. Every plunge rubbed spots inside that in turn lit nerves on fire in chain reactions throughout her body. Her breasts bounced as he rammed himself deep into her core, the broad expanse of his chest rubbing her now screamingly sensitive nipples on every stroke he delivered. Beth's world diminished to the sensory overload enclosed in the small chlorine-scented space.

Everything moved in slow motion as she opened her eyes and gazed into his. He returned her stare, his dark pupils mesmerizing, his wicked, sinful grin breaking at the corner of his mouth.

"Fucking against the wall. You ever done this before? Feel the cold of the concrete behind you, feel the heat of my cock as I ream you in two. It's good, ain't it darling? All for you. Every succulent, desirable..." He drove into her harder still, and alarms went off in the back of her brain. This wasn't going to be just an orgasm; it was going to be cataclysmic. "...every fuckable inch of you."

Her climax drew closer, hovering out of reach.

"Come for me again. I'm going to..." a deep-seated thrust, "...take you with me..." another, "...you feel so fucking good squeezing my cock..." another, "...come on, darling."

She came undone. Between the relentless strokes, the dirty talk and the whole naughtiness of the situation, the earth unraveled and took her with it. His mouth clamped down on hers as she started to cry out, the need to express the pleasure tearing her apart, overriding the logical sections of her brain. His tongue slammed into her mouth as his cock drilled her once again, and he jerked within her, his release shaking them both as he pinned her to the wall with his weight. Their kisses changed slowly, turning gentler, wet pleasure passing back and forth as their air exchanged—open mouths gasping against each other.

Daniel lowered her leg slowly. She let out a squeak of pain, the return of weight on the limb a stark contrast to the endorphins of pleasure racing through her. He soothed her, stroking his hand over her hip, kissing her forehead.

They were still connected intimately, his chest crushing her breasts. She swore his cock swelled even larger inside her, the skin of her passage unaccustomed to hard use for months. Hell, for years. Daniel kissed her again, dropping a line of tender caresses behind her ear, down her neck. His work-callused hands massaged her butt in smooth, rhythmic circles.

He let out a slow sigh. "We've got ten minutes' grace. I'm gonna head onto the deck. If you want to hit the change room, I'll round up the boys and herd them in your direction when they're done."

She still couldn't speak. He kissed her cheek, kissed her lips. When he pulled from her body, she shivered, sad at the loss of his heat. He twisted her around and sat her on the bench, stroking her cheek with his knuckles.

"You might want to hop in the shower for a minute."

She looked up at him, confused. Damn, he was fine. He dealt with the condom and pulled on his trunks, arranging his ample girth strategically.

"Beth? You gonna be okay?"

She pulled her towel over herself slowly, the rush of heat from the experience flushing her skin. "I'm fine. More than fine." She made herself speak. "Daniel?"

He turned in the act of unlocking the door. "Yeah?"

"Thank you."

He shook his head and grinned, and something inside came dangerously close to melting.

"Thank *you*. I've got to run."

She watched him walk out the door, then mustered up the strength to lock the door behind him before collapsing back onto the bench. Her head touched the wall behind her as she sucked in deep breathes of air. She'd really done it. They'd done it.

Non-vanilla.

Chapter Nine

"So you going to be able to make it to both the wedding and the party afterward?" Daniel tossed a few coins in the tip jar and turned to carry the coffees back to their table.

Their table, *sheesh.*

She was doing it again. She'd been fighting to make sure she kept her head on straight and didn't read too much into Daniel's attentive behaviour. He'd picked her up every day when she was done with classes and taken her out for a coffee. They had just enough time for a quick conversation to unwind before heading home to meet the bus at the gate. She still didn't feel comfortable talking in public about her past, but they seemed to have enough to chat about anyway. Now that October had begun, it seemed everyone was starting to get ready for the coming winter. They vented about her daily trials in the classroom and his on the ranch and in the Colemans' furniture workshop.

The adult company kept her sane. Oh yeah, hello, the addition of sex had rocked, and he was mighty easy on the eyes, but the companionship was another component she hadn't realized she craved so badly. This whole deal with Daniel was supposed to be about friendship and fun, not forever.

The part of her soul that occasionally wished that she'd found a man like Daniel in the first place? She wrapped that part up in ropes and tied it off real tight. It wasn't allowed to mess with the fantastic reality she was experiencing.

"Beth?"

She gazed into his eyes in confusion. "Sorry, wool gathering."

"No troubles. I asked if you're able to come to both the wedding and the reception. The boys are welcome."

Hadn't she told him? "Are you talking about Blake and Jaxi? This coming weekend?"

"Of course. The wedding is at—"

"Daniel, the boys and I are headed to Calgary on Friday after school lets out. We're spending Thanksgiving with my parents and my sister. I'm sorry, I thought I'd told you."

By the expression on his face, she hadn't, or he'd forgotten.

"That makes sense. You drive safe, and I'll see you when you get back."

He switched topics to describe a woodworking project he was making special order for a hotel in Canmore, and she fidgeted with her cup and tried to stay alert. She usually loved to listen to him, the rough timbre of his voice teasing all the spots in her psyche that needed a man's attention and sharing. In such a short time a piece of him had wrapped its way around her, and she was worried it would soon be impossible to not let it show.

"You think you'd like one?" he asked, and Beth stumbled to give an answer.

Somehow she got to the end of the visit without making too much more of a fool of herself. The tiny seed of hope in her heart she buried deep again, not letting it see any hint of light to encourage it. It was too soon to be thinking about getting seriously involved with another man. Heck, it hadn't even been a year since Samuel's death.

And although Daniel had been nothing but friendly and supportive, she hesitated to take it any further. She needed to stay in control. Call the shots.

It was the only way she knew she and the boys would remain safe.

Wasn't it?

The bright fall sunshine hit his eyes as Daniel passed another round of drinks to the tables then headed up the hill to spend some time alone, pondering why he wasn't particularly happy today. He found a seat on the warm grass, breathing in the scented air as he tried to relax. The crowd below him was loud and boisterous, celebrating the end of another growing season but more importantly the wedding of his oldest brother to their next-door neighbour's little girl. Jaxi was all grown up now, although it had taken a bit for that information to sink through Blake's thick skull.

Thanksgiving weekend was as appropriate a time as any for them to have held the wedding, only there was a pit in Daniel's belly. He should have been pleased. All his family was around, and it looked as if everyone was getting along. With six brothers, there had always been tough moments as they dealt with the reality of belonging to a big family. As six individuals they didn't always see eye to eye—yet for the most part they were tight.

The fact Beth had hauled her family back to Calgary for the weekend—*that* was the part that sucked. He hadn't realized how much he would miss her and the boys. He kept spotting things he wanted to show her, and his frustration made him irritable. He forced a smile on his face and tried to put her out of his mind.

"You planning on doing anything other than moping today,

big bro?"

His youngest brother smirked from where he had dropped by Daniel's feet, joining him on the grass. Joel wore that wide-eyed expression that made the girls flutter around like butterflies.

"Stick it, Joel."

Another chuckle sounded on his other side and Daniel groaned. Great, his quiet retreat space been invaded by the twins.

"Methinks someone is in love. His sweet princess is not here and he's got no one to dazzle." Jesse poked Joel in the ribs, the two of them sprawled lazily on the ground.

Daniel was tempted to smack their two heads together. "Idiots. Don't you have things you're supposed to do?"

Joel pointed to the outdoor dance area. "All set to go. Can't start anything else without the stars, and they're taking a powder break."

With a wiggle of his brow, Jesse gave a snort. "Probably trying to figure out a way to work in a quickie before they have to—"

"Do you mind?" *Holy shit*, but Jesse was annoying at times.

Joel whacked his twin on the arm and rolled him down the hill in the direction of the bar. "I see more customers for you. Quit being a jerk, if you can help it."

Jesse scrambled to his feet, then brushed himself off. He flipped Joel the bird behind his back as he good-naturedly headed to the bar area. Daniel shook his head and Joel laughed out loud.

"He's a pain in the ass, ain't he?"

Daniel raised a brow. "Like you aren't?"

"I know...two peas in a pod."

Daniel had to smile. Of all the six brothers, he was probably the closest with Joel, even with the whole twins-living-in-each-other's-pocket deal.

"You do seem like you're not all there today, and I don't think it's because you're upset Jaxi's joining the family." Joel pulled at the grass like a kid.

"I'm not the one who wanted to get involved with her. How are you doing?" Daniel watched the crowds of community folk that had come out for the wedding wander over the lawn area outside the sprawling main house of Six Pack Ranch.

Joel laughed. "Don't try to change the topic. We were talking about the fact the lady you've been visiting with daily isn't anywhere to be seen."

Daniel shrugged. "Couldn't be helped."

"You really like her, don't you?"

Daniel thought about it. First reaction? "Yeah. I do."

Joel's quick gaze darted around the crowd celebrating on the lawn. "So we going to see you doing this kind of thing before long?"

Oh hell. "That might be a touch difficult. She doesn't think of me that way." The expression of shock on his brother's face made a laugh burst out.

"Fuck, no—are you sure about that?"

"Fuck, yes."

Joel shook his head. "But I've been hearing all kinds of stories around town about you taking her out all the time and shit like that. What's going on if it's not you working your way up to proposing to the woman down the road? You said you'd had enough of the casual route after the whole fiasco with Sierra."

The reminder of his ex-girlfriend was enough to turn his

stomach. "It's not as easy as all that, Joel. Beth's a widow—she's got the kids and—" The way Joel glared at him made him talk twice as fast. "It's not that I don't like the kids..."

"Glad you didn't try to bullshit me on that one. You know you sure as hell can't make me believe you're not the least bit excited about not only finding a woman who's a knockout, but one who's got kids."

Daniel ran a hand through his hair. Why did that topic have to come up again? "I don't want to talk about that right now—"

"You told her yet? I mean, the fact you can't have kids was Sierra's reason for calling it off, wasn't it?"

He flicked at a speck of dirt on his pants. "Shit, Joel. Beth and I have only been seeing each other for a short while. It's not as if I'm going to up and announce, 'Hey, by the way, you know you don't have to worry about me getting you pregnant since I only shoot blanks.'"

Joel grunted, his face screwed up in disgust. "When you put it that way..." He shook his head for a second then checked his watch as he rose to his feet. "Damn, I need to get ready. Jaxi will kick my ass if I haven't got the dance music lined up."

"She and Blake do look good together, don't they?" Daniel stood as well, ready to head over to visit with his mom for a while.

"Yeah. I guess Jaxi did know which of us was best for her in the long run." Joel punched him in the shoulder then set out whistling down the path. Daniel took a moment to center himself. His family was all around. Matt and Travis had smoke rising from the barbecues. Jesse's grin flashed as he sweet-talked the girls congregating around the bar area. Daniel stared toward where his mama sat chatting with the bride's parents.

His big happy family. What he'd always known and enjoyed

105

and secretly hated at the same time. The beauty of the ranch and the never-ending chores. The support of family and the unceasing noise. It was a blessing and a curse.

At what point could what he wanted and loved—family and caring—be separated from what he'd had enough of?

Living on the ranch was wearing him down. Tearing him apart, and he just didn't know what to do about it. The small town? Not a problem, but he didn't want to be mucking out stalls and driving tractors for the rest of his life. He didn't have the grades to go back to school the way twins were doing. So here he was, trapped in a way. Trapped in the middle of love and caring, and he felt like the most ungrateful creature around that he wasn't as pleased and happy as he should be.

If only he could find a way to work with his hands to make a living, without being held captive by the whim of the weather and the animals. If he knew for sure there was a future for him that involved a family, in spite of the fact he couldn't have any kids himself.

He wasn't sure what drew him to Beth, although it wasn't the fact she had kids. His fascination had begun before he'd made that discovery. The lost expression in her eyes when she didn't think anyone was looking. The way she squared her shoulders and took a deep breath before barrelling forward in the direction she thought she should go.

He wished he understood better what haunted her, but every time he tried to turn the conversation in that direction, it seemed the topic got changed.

She was running, he was searching.

Maybe part of what they needed was each other.

He headed back down toward the celebrations, wishing Beth were here, the boys racing around in circles with the other children. The wish made his heart ache even more.

Beth sat quietly, staring into her coffee cup.

"You want another piece of pie?"

She lifted her head and made herself laugh. "Holy cow, Mom, you want me to roll home tomorrow?" Her mom smiled and pulled out the chair next to her. Plopping her elbows on the table, she turned and asked the question Beth had been dreading all weekend.

"So, how are you really doing?"

Could she answer without answering? Beth opened her mouth and her mom cut her off.

"Sweetie, don't try to pull a fast one on me either. I had enough of your lies during the time you were married to Samuel. I'm not going to let you slip one past me again."

The pain in her mother's eyes was real. "Mom, none of what happened to me was your fault."

"Well, it wasn't yours either, but you still had to go through it. The fact you didn't tell any of us that Samuel had changed so much over the years—"

"Mom." Beth rose, ready to escape, but her mom laid a hand on her arm.

"Stay. I'm sorry, I won't bring it up again. I need to know...are you doing okay? The boys talked through the meal about friends at school and all kinds of things they've been enjoying. Sounds as if they've settled into the community the way you hoped."

The boys rambling during dinner had been a saving grace. She hadn't been forced to add anything to the conversation, just smile and pass the food from one side of the table to the other. Her big happy family. Grandma and Grandpa doting on the boys, and her sister and her new boyfriend laughing together about something. Beth managed to ignore the happiness radiating from Darleen like a neon light.

She thought she'd had love in the beginning with Samuel.

"Rocky's been good. In some ways the fire in the apartment house was a blessing since the house where we ended up has been fabulous to live in. I'm not looking forward to having to move again in a few months."

Her mom spoke firmly. "I think you should ask for an extension. Wait until the spring to move. Shifting stuff in the winter isn't a lot of fun."

Beth shook her head. "Us living there has already put the older Coleman boys into a tough situation. I'm grateful for how giving the whole family has been, but I don't want to take advantage of their goodwill."

"You know, there's times it's not goodwill or charity, it's because people can see it's the right thing to do. Have you thought of that?"

The sad part was her mom was probably right. Mike had already told her there was no rush for her to move, but she still felt uncomfortable.

Her mom folded her hands in her lap. "Tell me about Daniel. The boys seem to think a lot of him. He's an instructor at the swimming pool, right?"

Beth snorted. "Where'd you get that idea?" Daniel would get a kick out his new profession.

"The boys said he takes them swimming every Saturday. I figured they were in lessons or something." Her mom's eyes narrowed and Beth blushed. "He's not an instructor. Beth, are you seeing someone?"

"No." The word shot out so fast she surprised herself.

Mom raised a brow. "Okay."

"I'm not." Her cheeks heated even more, and she scrambled for what to say to throw her suddenly very attentive mother off the track.

"All right. Relax. If you're not ready to talk about it, that's fine. But I was going to remind you that if at some point you get involved with someone and need a few days alone, you give me a call. Grandma has wheels and loves to travel."

She forced her mouth closed. In spite of the fact her mother was close to the truth, Beth had no desire to confess anything quite yet. "Mom, what do you think I'm doing out in Rocky Mountain House?"

"Hopefully you're starting to live a little again. Doctor said you could leave the brace off more often, right?"

"What does my brace have to do with...?" Beth bit her lips. She was not going to continue this conversation. She was twenty-nine years old and talking about sex with her mother had stopped when she was sixteen.

Mom rose and grabbed the coffeepot, refilling both their cups. She sat back down and let out a huge sigh. "I know you don't want to talk about it, but I'm going to talk and you can listen. Honey, you lived with an abusive man for ten years and kept it from us for most of that time. Now that he's gone, you've been making changes I think most women with your history would be afraid to attempt. You're taking charge of your life and trying to make sure you've got nothing but the best happening for your boys."

Her mom reached over and clasped their hands together. "I applaud your decision to make a fresh start in a small town, even though it means you and the boys are farther away from me. I want to help, okay? I love you, and you deserve to smile again like you used to when you were young. You are one of the strongest people I know, no matter what Samuel used to tell you. You are beautiful and trustworthy and valuable, and I'm very, very proud of you."

Beth watched with tear-filled eyes as her mom squeezed her fingers then fussed at the table for a moment before sipping from her coffee cup. Silence surrounded them as Beth took her time to process what her mom had shared. The shattered pieces of the past had cut everyone involved, and the lacerations went far and deep.

"You're proud of me?" She sniffed and wiped her mouth, taking a deep breath to slow her pounding heart.

Her mom nodded. "Very."

Beth closed her eyes and soaked in the familiar sounds of family. The boys' laughter, their Grandpa's deeper boom and the noise of the television mixed together and poured from the room next door in a kind of harmonic soundtrack to her life.

Her world had changed so much from the rose-coloured future she'd imagined as a newlywed. Samuel's demands rose so slowly that she wasn't even aware he was abusing her. Controlling her, yes, then making her dread making a mistake. He'd never physically threatened the boys, but they had quickly learned when it was time to stay out of sight and sound of their father.

And when the day came he finally hit her...

Beth stared out the window. There were a few leaves left clinging to the branches. Brown dead things swinging in the breeze. She was tired of being dead.

Daniel made her feel alive.

"Daniel is..." She puffed air, her bangs wiggling. "He's special." Beth lifted her gaze to see her mom smiling, the corners of her mouth twisted a tiny bit.

"You seeing him?"

Beth shook her head at first then grudgingly shrugged. "Kind of. He's been around a fair bit. Supportive, caring, fabulous with the boys."

"Good looking?"

"Oh, Mom, you want a physical dossier?"

Her mom grinned. "Why yes, yes I would. So if he's not an instructor at the pool, what's he do?"

"He's one of the Coleman boys, from the ranch next door."

The smile on her mom's face faded. "Oh."

Beth frowned. "What's that supposed to mean?"

Mom wiggled her nose. "I see why you said you felt as if you were taking advantage of them." She took another drink before putting the cup down firmly. "Still, there's nothing wrong with it. You feel...comfortable around him?"

Beth flushed at the thought of the last time they were together. Comfortable? Oh yeah. She dragged her mind out of the gutter and concentrated on what her mom was really asking.

"I took it slow at first, only seeing him in public, but he's been nothing but trustworthy. He's actually very gentle. It's kind of confusing. Even when Samuel was nice, you know at the beginning, he always added that underlying 'I'm the man, you're the woman, my way or the highway' component to our relationship."

"Daniel doesn't do that?"

Beth hesitated. "He's confident, and a naturally take charge kind of guy, but I never feel as if he's pushing too hard. It's like what he wants the most is what I want."

Her mom made one of those *hmm* type sounds. "Then I'm going to be even nosier and ask. If you feel comfortable around him, are you planning on giving him a real chance? Or is this going to be something that you need more time on?" She shook her finger in Beth's direction. "Don't make that face at me. You know what I'm talking about. After all those years fighting, striving to keep your identity when all Samuel wanted to do was make you into the image he wanted to see...it's got to be hard to know when you can really trust a person."

Beth lost the logic in that one. "You think I can't trust him?"

"I didn't say that. I said maybe *you* think you can't trust him. Or anyone except yourself, yet. There's a time coming when you have to expand your radius of trust farther than simply your father and me. I'm not suggesting this man is someone you're going to be with forever. I don't know anything about him except what you've just told me. Still, you need to think about it. If he does become someone you want around more permanently, you'll have to show him that you're ready."

It was a lot to consider, so all Beth did was nod, then come around the table to give her mom the biggest hug possible.

A soft pat landed on her cheek. "Now, about another matter. We were wondering if you wanted to have Christmas at your place. Then you won't have to drive the winter roads with your bad leg and the three boys. I worry about you on the highway."

In one swoop, she was back to being the child and her mom taking care of her. "Mom, it's only a couple of hours."

"We'd love to see where you've landed. You didn't want any help getting settled and I can respect that, but for Christmas, we want to come to you."

They ironed out the details and another small section of the ice in her heart thawed. It would be their first Christmas without Samuel. Having a house full of family and being in a new location would be a good thing.

Chapter Ten

The light tapping on the door made her heart start pounding. Every time she swore she wasn't going to let it happen and it still did.

Beth opened the door then frowned in confusion.

"Hey, Ms. Danube."

Instead of Daniel, whom she'd expected, the tenth-grade student who usually babysat for her stood there, backpack slung over one shoulder. The girl slipped into the house and peeled off her bag and jacket, looking around the house in anticipation. "Where're the boys?"

"They're upstairs getting their pyjamas on. Sandy, why...?"

"Beth." The door opened again, and Daniel stepped in, his eyes flashing as he swept a glance over her body that heated her up in an instant. "Sandy's going to babysit for the evening, if that's okay. I have something I want to show you."

Sandy called out from the kitchen. "You want them in bed at the usual time, Ms. D?"

Beth answered without thinking, watching Daniel stalk her across the room. That was the only way to describe what he was doing. He took slow, deliberate steps toward her, his heated gaze melting her defences. Then he was standing right there, inches away from her body.

She yearned to touch him.

"I want to kiss you," he whispered. "I *need* to kiss you."

She glanced at the stairs. The boys would be down in only seconds, but if this relationship had any chance of moving on, like her mom had suggested, maybe it was time to see how the boys reacted.

She tilted her head back and leaned in, letting him close the final distance between them so their lips could touch. Light. Gentle, a simple press together that still made her body sing.

They drew apart before anyone arrived. Except the fact she'd initiated the kiss, here where they could get caught—he'd noticed. He beamed at her and stepped back. "Hey, no brace. Doctor say things are fine?"

There were two questions in his voice. "My leg is doing much better. He wants me to use the brace as little as possible. And everything else is good too." No condoms needed anymore, if that was the other part of what he was asking.

The smile on his face grew. "That's great about your leg. I bet it will make it easier to get around, but you be sure to let me know if I ever need to help you, okay? Oh, and me too." He pulled a folded paper from his pocket, displaying the edge.

They stared at each other for a minute. Beth tried to decide if the X-rated thoughts racing through her mind made her evil or if it was a good sign.

"You got a coat?"

She nodded, curious what he was up to. The boys poured down the stairs and surrounded him, shrieks of joy ringing out at his presence.

"Daniel. You going to read to us?"

"Did you see my bruise? It's huge."

Beth held on to the back of a chair as Daniel gave complete attention to the trio of wet-headed boys. He knelt down and talked to each in turn, and Beth shook her head to fight off the urge to picture this more permanently. That was too soon and not what she'd asked for.

Her heart didn't care.

Daniel stood. "Well, guys, that's all very fascinating, but you know what? I'm not here tonight to see you. I'm stealing your mama away for a bit, so Sandy is going to take care of you."

Lance narrowed his eyes, and Beth held her breath as she wondered how he'd react. "You going on a date?"

Daniel looked at her, waiting for her to respond. Letting her make the decision of what was said. Three more pairs of eyes stared her direction and she hesitated for a second. Damn it, it wasn't fair to anyone to hold off on moving forward. She smiled brightly. "Yeah, it's a date."

Her littlest one wrinkled up his face. "Mommies don't date."

Beth laughed. "It's a way of saying we're friends and we want to spend some grown-up time together. Sandy is here to take care of you."

Nathan tugged on Daniel's sleeve. "You still going to be our friend and play with us?"

"Of course."

That was enough for him. Nathan bounced off, dragging Robbie out of Beth's arms where he'd crawled for a kiss.

Lance exited the room slower, staring over his shoulder, and Beth hesitated. Looked like her oldest son was having the most trouble with the idea, but any conversation with him would have to wait until the morning.

He led her through the trees, rubbing her hand with his fingers where it lay on his arm. The leaves underfoot crackled as they stepped through them, tall grasses lying flat on the ground and the smell of winter coming closer. They walked in silence for the longest time, and Daniel wondered how best to continue their discussion.

Beth tugged lightly on his arm, and he slowed, turning her to face him. The warmth of her body spread, flowing over his limbs and driving into his heart.

"You okay with what I told the boys?" she asked.

He lifted her chin and took her lips under his. She tasted sweet and needy, pressing closer to him like she wanted to weld them into one skin. He'd already decided he had to know where they were headed in the future. Maybe not asking her now, this instant, but soon.

"I told you from the start I wanted to see you for more than just sex. Although there's some wicked memories running through my brain—"

"Me too." She grabbed his face in her hands and grinned up at him. "I have no idea how you came up with that shower scheme, but holy smokes. You don't know how hot the whole situation was for me. How freeing and so much what I needed right then."

He stared into her eyes, the sincerity and intensity of what she said clear. Still...

"It wasn't very romantic." If he could pick her up and carry her to the king-sized bed in her room, he would be in heaven. Cover her with his body and bury himself deep while he watched her face every second.

There were some positive things about sex with a lady flat on her back.

She snickered. "It was totally hot, and I told you before I've done romantic and I've done slow. What I'm looking for is more. You delivered, totally and completely."

116

"Really?"

She slapped his shoulder. "Yes, really. I want to know what you've got planned for an encore."

"Your wish is my desire." Daniel tilted his head to indicate their direction.

She glanced down the trail in confusion. "Sex outdoors? Okay..." Her enthusiasm faded, and he laughed.

"It's a little chilly for that, don't you think?"

"I'm game."

"I think I can figure out something else that's not vanilla but still warm. Come on." He tucked her under his arm and kissed her temple before guiding her through the trees.

They broke into the open just past the barns and outbuildings, close to where the heavy equipment was lined up neatly for the night. He sensed Beth's confusion as they continued to walk, as he guided her over the rough sections of trail to where the small guest cabin sat behind the main house. He opened the door and led her in.

"This is where Jaxi lives, isn't it?"

"Jaxi and Blake, but they're on their honeymoon. They'll be home next weekend. I cleaned it out a little and we're good. They won't mind at all."

Beth raised an eye at him. "There's a bed in here."

"Don't hold it against me."

"Don't hold me against it..."

He laughed. Damn, he loved her sense of humour. "I told you, I have a million things I want to do with you. It's warm and cozy and private here. You ready to play?"

Her grin lit up the room.

"I need to know one thing. When you said you wanted to try

it all...did that mean just me playing with you? 'Cause, darling, I have to confess I have this one dream that's making my body ache and if you're interested..."

Her gaze dropped to his crotch. His cock rose in response, creating a bulge in the fabric.

Her tongue darted out briefly as she wet her lips. "You want me to touch you?"

"Oh yeah."

She shrugged out of her coat and tossed it on the chair beside the door. The top two buttons of her blouse had slipped opened, and he swallowed, shifting his hips to try to ease the pressure now flooding his groin. If he didn't get her sweet mouth on his cock soon he was going to explode right in his fucking jeans.

"I've never given anyone—I mean, I've never done it before." She straightened her spine. "I'm interested...if you're willing to teach me."

"I think I could handle that." He undid his button, her gaze lowering to watch, her pupils growing huge. She licked her lips again as he unzipped and his cock sprang free.

"You're not wearing any underwear."

"It's called commando, darling, and usually it's fine." He took himself in hand, slipping from tip to root as he pushed his jeans farther open. "Only when I'm around you, it increases the danger. I swear I've got the imprint of the zipper on my cock."

She stepped closer and reached for him. He let her wrap her hand around him, holding in the swear words wanting to burst out, it felt so fucking good. Hesitant strokes up and down teased him. When she brought her other hand to touch his balls through the fabric of his jeans, he sucked in air.

"You're killing me." She flipped her head up, her breathing

hard, almost as uneven as his. "You like touching me?"

"Yes. My husband..."

He leaned in and swallowed the words. With her hands on his cock, there was no way he wanted to be talking about that man. This was about her and him, and nobody else. When they drew apart, he covered her fingers, stopping the torment as she'd continued to explore. "Let me lose the jeans, and we'll go on." He looked her over. "You want to take off your blouse and bra too? 'Cause I love watching you."

Her face flushed, but she loosened the extra buttons one at a time. He couldn't look away as the fabric floated apart to reveal her soft skin, the rosy flush of desire covering her neck and the firm swell of her breasts peeking out from under the lace of her bra. The very pretty and delicate yellow bra.

"You went shopping in Calgary, didn't you?" He pressed open her blouse, sliding his hands over the warm skin of her waist, lifting upward until his palms rested over the pale material hiding her breasts.

Beth grinned. "You're not allowed to cut this one off me."

"Hmm. Leave it on, I'll enjoy looking at you like this too."

He stripped off his T-shirt and shucked his jeans, keeping his gaze firmly on her to enjoy every minute. The minx put on a show, shrugging her shoulders and letting the fabric fall to the floor behind her. She stretched her arms in the air, and her breasts rose, the tight nipples stabbing the lace and forming tiny ridges. When she reached for her jeans, he held out a hand to stop her.

"Later. Sit."

He helped her settle on the edge of the low bed. For some reason, Blake and Jaxi had their mattress and box spring resting on the floor. It must have made it awkward for getting in and out of bed, but there was one very obvious advantage.

119

Beth's eyes widened as she stared at his now-eye-level cock. "Damn."

He chuckled. "Yeah, damn. Right now it's all about me." He watched her closely as he stepped between her thighs, his dick aimed at her like an arrow at a target.

Beth tilted her head up and smiled at him. "Can't be all about you when I'm the one who wants to try. What do I do?"

Anything you want. "Hold me. That's right. Now lick the head." She leaned forward and slipped out the tip of her tongue, tasting him. He was going to die. Her tentative touch sent a jolt of lightning through his entire body.

"Oh, you taste..." that sweet smile flashed again, "...good." She swirled her tongue around the crown of his cock, warm wetness coating him, and he swore softly. The urge to thrust into her mouth was powerful but he held back, wanting her to enjoy this as much as he was. She opened wide and enveloped him, and his heart skipped a beat.

"Hell, that's it. Get me good and wet. Use your tongue while you, oh shit, yeah..." She was a damn quick learner. She sucked and pulled back, her teeth lightly grazing his flesh, and he hardened impossibly. It wasn't going to take much to set him off tonight. Watching made every sensation more intense.

With tentative nibbles, she set his heart pounding. The delicate rasp of her tongue on the tender underside of his shaft sent an icy tingle up his spine. She explored with her lips, her fingers, cupping his balls and rolling them lightly, and he squeezed his eyes closed and fought for control.

Maybe she'd never gone down on a man before, but sweet mercy, if she wasn't doing everything exactly right.

He lowered a hand to stroke his fingers through her hair, loving the way the curls shone in the light, the way their softness caressed his palm. He cupped her cheek for a second, brushing his thumb against the edge of her mouth. Touching where they intimately connected.

She slipped her lips farther down his shaft, and the crown of his cock nudged the back of her throat. Her eyes popped open, and she gagged for a second. "Ease off, sweetheart. Only go as far as you want."

Daniel tried to retreat, not offer as much of his length, but she let go of where she'd grasped his cock and grabbed both cheeks of his ass. Her fingernails dug into his skin like a kitten's. His cock jerked in reaction and she hummed.

He was a second and a half from all hell breaking loose.

"Darling, you need to decide if you want me to come in your mouth or not." *Decide fucking fast too.* Beth pulled him toward her, his cock spreading her lips wide, the moisture from his precome and her saliva coating him and shining in the light of the room. Another rock of his hips, and another, fucking her mouth slowly but firmly as she willingly lapped and sucked.

"Beth, I'm going to come." His balls drew tight, the tingling sensation at the root of his cock nearly numbing him. She flicked a glance upward, a sweet smile curving the edge of her lips where they stretched around him, and he lost it. A jet of come shot from his tip into her mouth, and she lurched down again, swallowing involuntarily. The additional suction blew his mind and dragged out another jolt of semen. Beth pulled back, and he slipped from her lips, still coming. A strand flew out to land in her open mouth, another to lie in a sticky string along her cheek. "Fuck, that's hot."

Beth laughed aloud and opened wider, reaching with her tongue to try and recapture him.

Daniel grabbed his cock and pumped a few more times, aiming at her mouth as he shot the rest of his load. She yanked him close, pinching his butt until she once again enveloped the softening length of his shaft. She swallowed and he swore. It felt so bloody amazing his legs grew weak. He stood on shaky limbs for a moment until his cock grew too sensitive for her continuing exploration.

She protested when he withdrew, squatting down to stare into her eyes.

"I was having fun," she complained. She poked out her tongue to gather some of the semen from her cheek, and he sucked for air.

"Damn it, woman, you undo me."

"Was I any good?"

Oh yeah. "Any better and I'd be dead." He touched her cheek, and her hand flew up to find the moisture there. A blush rolled over her skin, and he dropped to his knees between her thighs. "Hell, don't be embarrassed. Do you have any idea how much that turns me on? To see you marked with my come?"

She snickered and ran her hand through his hair, her eyes dancing over his face, his torso. "I'm a mess. Tasted different than I thought it would." Her gaze met his, heat behind the stare. "What's next? My turn?"

"Damn right. I need a few minutes to recover. You got any requests?"

"You're doing pretty good without any suggestions on my part."

He helped her out of her jeans and undies, holding himself back from attacking her. A long, slow stare from bottom to top whet his appetite for much, much more. "Hmm, you're so damn beautiful. Crawl yourself up on the bed and grab hold of the headboard."

Chapter Eleven

Confusion painted her expression for a second before she complied. Her slow crawl over the bed's surface gave him a chance to watch her, gauge how easily she manoeuvred. The range of motion in her injured leg improved all the time. That fact made him warm inside. He hated the flashes of pain marring her eyes when something bumped her the wrong way.

Damn. She knelt, legs spread wide, hands clutching the headboard. Her knuckles grew white as he circled the side of the bed to drag the pillows off the mattress, clearing the space between her legs.

"You planning on tearing the wood apart, darling?"

"Just not sure what you're up to." A slight tremor shook her voice, and he hurried to reassure her. He stroked a hand down her spine, over the curve of her ass. Soft smooth skin, goose bumps rising beneath his touch.

"I won't do anything you don't like. Remember, you're in total control here." He slipped his hand down and cupped her pussy. The curls covering her were wet. "You got excited sucking me off, didn't you?"

"Yes."

He slid a finger into her sheath and she gasped.

"Hmm, very excited. You're dripping." He crowded her, rubbing his chest against her back, the length of his cock nestled in the crease of her ass. He nibbled on her neck, licking her earlobe as she leaned her head to the side.

"More..."

"More what?" She tasted so good. He scraped his teeth down the tendon, her shivering body making him respond faster than he thought possible. His cock headed rapidly back to full steam. "Touching you? Like this?"

He slid his hand up, drawing the cream of her body toward her anus. When he rimmed the tiny hole she swore, tightening around his finger.

"Oh God, you're not going to...?" She might have protested, but her body said otherwise, her hips pressing back toward him.

He slipped his finger past the tight muscle up to the first knuckle, just to torment himself. "Not this instant, but yeah, I want to." He nuzzled her neck. "You want me to fuck your ass, don't you? You curious?"

She nodded.

Hot damn. "Maybe next time. Right now, I have other plans." He dropped to his back and slid under her, covering her pussy with his mouth. She shouted with surprise.

The position was perfect, and he took advantage of the easy access to both her pussy and her ass, squeezing her cheeks, massaging hard then smoothing circles over her heated skin. All the while he explored her depths with his tongue, lapping eagerly. The sounds of passion from her lips encouraged him to flick her clit harder, the bud swelling under his ministrations. He wet a finger in his mouth and drew a line down her ass again and again, rubbing the rosette of her anus until she rocked against his hand. Once she was slick enough, he pressed firmly, spearing her between his hand and his tongue. She screamed and came.

"Holy hell, you're responsive. You're not supposed to be able to come that quick. Give me another."

"I can't believe you've got your... Oh God."

He didn't let up. He buried his tongue as deep as he could and set up a smooth pace with his finger in her ass. Fucking her like that, tasting her response in his mouth felt so bloody good, he thought he was going to come again without a single touch to his once-again rock-solid cock.

She might have complained about being inexperienced, but in reality her reactions were perfect—just what he liked in a woman. The shy, flirty glances contrasted with the wild cat. She was so receptive to everything he suggested. Every time he touched her, she held back nothing. And the noises she made— holy fuck, the squeals and moans made the whole situation way hotter than if she'd stayed quiet. He latched on to her clit and suckled, pulling the tender nub between his lips and pulsing in time with the assault on her ass.

"Yes, right there. Please, just a little more..." The words faded away into a keen of pleasure as she came. Like a whirlwind above him, Beth blew apart. Her whole body shook, ass tightening around his finger. Her cream dropped to his mouth, hot and sweet, her passion unmistakable.

He continued to lap, slower now, softer. Slipping his tongue between her folds and licking her clean. The frantic motions she'd been making calmed. When he pulled his finger from her ass, she moaned and leaned her hips back awkwardly to make eye contact.

"You're amazing. How did you come up with this one?"

Daniel kissed the inside of her thighs one after another then tugged until she sat on his chest. She protested, but he held her in place until she settled, the weight of her body so good on top of him.

"Since you've not led a checkered past, I guess you've never experienced a moustache ride before."

Beth laughed. "That's what that was? Okay, not exactly how I pictured it."

"Well, I don't have a moustache, so it doesn't really count. But good?"

She brushed his chest with her fingertips. Contentment shone on her face and that pleased him no end. "Very good."

He massaged her hips, a soft touch, stroking her with tender caresses. "You ready for more?"

She glanced at the clock on the wall. "We've got lots of time left."

"I still have something to show you."

"Really? I thought that was a ploy to get me out of the house so we could come here for sex."

"It was, kind of."

He shifted her, sitting beside her on the mattress. There could be no doubt he was interested in more action, his cock fully erect and rising into the air. She touched him again, her continued fascination clear. He let her explore at her own pace, all the while wondering what the hell kind of man she'd been married to who didn't take advantage of the fire and blistering-hot passion the woman was capable of.

Only this was not the time or place for that conversation. He was going to have it soon though. Putting off the topic helped neither of them. Until they both spoke honestly—about a whole bunch of things—there wasn't much chance of this relationship going anywhere important.

He was more and more determined important was what he wanted.

He sucked in a breath as Beth leaned over and nibbled on

his skin, just above his left nipple.

"So does your aversion to the bed include lying on your stomach?" he asked.

Beth dropped a trail of kisses over his chest, letting her fingers tangle in the dusting of hair. Teasing down to his belly button and southward to his cock. "The bed is fine. You know what I wanted to avoid, and if I can mention, so far you are doing simply excellent in your choices."

She was tickling him lightly when he grabbed her wrists in one hand to still them.

The instant fear that swept her came from nowhere, shocking in its arrival and its strength. *It was her wrists.* Icy dread raced through her, and she gasped, her body freezing in position. Daniel quickly let her loose, but there was no hiding how out of place with their circumstances her response had been.

"Beth? You okay?"

Her heart pounded, and she concentrated on breathing slowly to control her reaction. Concentrating on the facts helped—he'd done nothing wrong. He wasn't Samuel about to punish her for failing to reach some unnamed standard. He wasn't restraining her to take a swing.

Oh dear, would the fear ever totally be gone?

Beth lifted her chin. She had to keep moving forward. Daniel was a good man, a trustworthy man, and she didn't want to allow the evils of the past rule her life. Pushing aside everything but how excited Daniel made her feel, she scrambled for control.

"You surprised me." Deliberately, she lowered herself to the mattress then rolled over carefully to her belly. She swung her head to examine him over her shoulder. "Is this what you want?"

Her level of arousal had diminished, but she bet he could bring her back up quickly.

Daniel nodded. It looked as if he wanted to say more, and she prayed he'd ignore her momentary lapse. He stroked a hand down the length of her body, starting at her neck, skimming her shoulder blades, along the side of her waist. The gentle caress reignited all kinds of sensitive nerves, and her sex tingled again, moisture leaking from her. Two orgasms weren't enough with this man. The motion of his hand carried over the swell of her butt before lightly tracing the scars on her thigh.

She suddenly realized he'd never said a word about the visual damage marring her body, not a single time they'd been at the swimming pool together.

"Does it bother you? To see how scarred up my leg is?"

"Hell, no. It only bothers me that the accident must have hurt like blue blazes. I think you're very beautiful, Beth, and there's no way a few lines will change my opinion."

She flushed at his compliment, and her heart warmed even more.

He straddled her hips and massaged her back, thumbing the tight muscles along her spine until they loosened. The temperature in the cabin was perfect for her bare skin, and she relaxed. The sexual buzz in her body remained but more importantly her sense of well-being returned. Outdoors, faint murmurs rose on the air, the wind in the trees knocking branches against the roof. All the noises that sounded so frightening when she sat alone in the big house after the boys were in bed. Now they were a part of a symphony, a part of the sensory overload sweeping her.

Daniel leaned over and kissed the nape of her neck. "You

sure you want me to go on? I'm fine with stopping if you've had enough."

His skin slicked warmly against hers. His cock pressed her hip, the rigid shaft she wanted inside her body so much. "As if you aren't sitting there with a massive erection."

He dropped to the mattress beside her, staring into her eyes. An attempt to mind-read what she refused to share? "It won't kill me to wait. You already made me very happy once tonight."

The final edge of fear melted away completely. He was a decent man through and through. She pressed a palm against his firm body, loving the feel of him, so intimate and close. Did she want to stop? No way.

"I'm fine. Better than fine, and I really want you to continue with your nefarious plans."

"If you're sure." He took the time to kiss her thoroughly, a tender meeting of mouths and tongues, his hands cradling her head. She rolled to her side to let the warmth of his body touch hers. For a minute she truly forgot everything—the past, the troubles of balancing each day in the present, the worries about the future. There was nothing but sensation and sweet warmth, the clean scent of his skin and the taste of sin from his lips. He whispered in her ear, "Lift your hips."

She complied and he slid two pillows under her, raising her bottom high. The position wasn't uncomfortable, but a trifle undignified and very exposed.

"What are you doing?" she asked as he left her to dig in the backpack he'd brought along.

"Getting the things I wanted to show you."

"With my ass in the air..." What was the man up to now? He had already said they weren't having anal sex today. *Shoot.* She swore before she even spotted the toys in his hand.

He lay on the bed beside her and chuckled. "You're a very smart woman."

She rose on one elbow to stare at the assortment of plastic displayed before her. Sex toys were a new experience. Samuel had never allowed her to have anything that could possibly challenge his manhood, and only months after she'd recovered from the accident had she worked up the courage to slip into an adult shop and blushingly make a purchase. Lying next to her were three intriguing items—a slim plastic vibrator, a rubbery one with small to bigger knobs and, if she wasn't mistaken, a string of anal beads. "Where did you find these? And please don't tell me here in Rocky."

Daniel continued to stroke her back as she picked up the items one at a time, checking them out. "There is a shop in town, but I didn't go there. I drove to Red Deer to get the blood work done. Figured that would give us more privacy than broadcasting to the whole community what we were up to. I spotted the shop and couldn't resist."

He kissed her cheek again, nuzzled her neck. "Enough talking. Close your eyes."

Beth let out a slow breath and returned the beads to the mattress. She lowered her head and suddenly every inch of her grew hypersensitive.

"Warn me before you use those things." Control. She wanted to maintain control, if only a minute amount.

He laughed, a warm, comforting sound. Pleasure slid across her skin with his touch, with the scent of his body so close.

He nibbled on her earlobe. "You made a list, remember? Of things you wanted to try?"

Her eyes popped open. Oh no, what had she written down? Had he seen it? "You said you didn't need to look at it..."

"Don't worry, I didn't snoop, but there are a few experiences I thought you might have suggested that I'm not comfortable with." He kissed her shoulder and crawled over her, heat rising again. "You remember what I told you about the twins?"

She swallowed, hard. It was not a thing most women would forget.

"Oh, yeah, you know what I'm saying. They have this reputation for sharing a woman between them. They are pretty damn vocal about it too, so when I started thinking about all the non-vanilla things there are to show you, it kinda popped into my head. Only I realized there was no way on earth I could arrange that experience for you."

With his tongue, he traced a line from her ear to between her shoulder blades, and she shivered under his lips.

She cleared her throat, her voice coming out husky, and his cock jerked where it rested against her thigh. "Two guys at once. You don't think it's a good idea?"

"Oh, it's very good for the lady, but I'm afraid I've got a couple of troubles with doing anything like that with you. I've tried it before, and it can be hot. But when you're with me, I'm the one responsible for your pleasure. I'm greedy." He nipped her ass and she vibrated with need. "I want to know that what you're feeling is because of my hands. My mouth, my cock."

Delight bubbled up inside her and she couldn't stop the laughter. "Your toys?"

He hummed in agreement. "Damn right."

Then the room got quiet, except for the sound of their breathing. His hands seemed to be everywhere at the same time. The scent of vanilla rose into the air as a warm slickness touched her skin. Daniel lifted the slim vibrator from the bed and clicked it on, the soft buzz loud in the silence of the room.

He trailed the tip along her back, over her buttocks, dipping the rigid length between her cheeks and running all the way down to her most sensitive spots. He turned it on real low and arranged the vibrator lengthwise to lean against her sex, not inside her sheath, merely nestled between her labia and over the hood of her clit.

The continual gentle motion made the blood pound between her legs. A tingle started deep inside, and she held her breath, waiting to see what was next.

It wasn't long in coming. Daniel's firm hands landed on her butt, massaging and squeezing. He separated the cheeks of her ass and drew a fingertip over her anus, and she tightened involuntarily.

"Shh, don't worry. I'll go slow." Again and again he stroked, smooth liquid coating his fingers, easing his way. She forced aside all the thoughts about how wrong she'd always been told this was and instead concentrated on how very right it felt. Each time she relaxed a little more, her body melting into the bed, he praised her. When he rubbed his fingertip in one spot and she stayed open to his seeking touch, he leaned over and kissed her.

Something unfamiliar touched her skin, and she cracked open an eye to see the bumpy vibrator was missing. Another touch to her anus, still gentle, nothing more than the size of his fingertip.

He pressed harder and the tight ring of muscle guarding her stretched wider, then relaxed. Oh God, he pushed steadily, inching the larger and larger swells into her. She breathed slowly, trying to keep from tightening.

Then there were too many sensations at once. Daniel removed the second vibrator from between her legs, the absence making her crave a touch. Something wet and hot covered her as he licked her now ultrasensitive clit.

The tingling sensation rocketed off low. The contrast with the aching need in her sex and the unfamiliar burn in her butt made her breath catch. Another inch, another stretch, and finally Daniel's hand rested firmly on her backside. He kissed his way up her body until his lips hovered over her ear.

"I'm so fucking hard right now after watching that toy sink into your ass. There's no way I could bear to have anyone touch you like that in front of me, so you're going to have to pretend." The toy rocked, wiggling inside, and it felt so damn good she wanted... She didn't know what she wanted anymore. There was nothing but raw sensation left, and when he clicked a button and the vibration began again, this time inside her ass, she cried out with pleasure.

"Daniel, please..."

He crawled back between her legs, and she pulled her good leg up, opening to him. He dragged his cock against her wet center then with one smooth motion, buried himself deep.

Oh my God, the heft of his shaft filled her like never before. With the toy in her ass and his cock in her sex, a climax rushed forward with a frightening speed. The thumping and throbbing was more than blood rushing through her veins, it was every inch of her skin reacting to his possession.

And when he touched the vibrator in her ass, dragging it out a notch and thrusting it back in at the same time as he speared his hips forward, she was lost.

The orgasm went from explosive to unending. The initial blast made her squeeze his cock tight, and he swore, calling out her name as he plunged into her body. Aftershocks went off deep inside her core and in her ass, muscles pulsing around the vibrating toy.

There was nowhere to move, nowhere to go. Nothing to do

but feel as Daniel held her hips and slammed in. The speed of his thrusts picked up, the cant of his hips driving him deeper and deeper, and the pleasure seemed unending.

He grunted on each stroke, his pleasure clear. Suddenly he slowed, concern in his voice as he spoke. "Is that okay? Tell me if I'm being too rough."

Screw that, he wasn't too rough. If anything, this wasn't enough. Not nearly enough.

"Harder," she commanded. He reached under her to squeeze her clit between his fingertips, and the bolt of lightning that struck was so incredible she screamed. "Yes. Please. Harder."

"You need to come, darling. I need to feel you around me, so tight, so good."

He dragged her back as he thrust forward, slapping their thighs together, the sounds of grunts and groans and sheer decadent sex filling the room. Another orgasm hovered, volatile, dangerous.

Fiery.

Daniel swept over her clit, but this time he pressed his fingertips hard on the aching bundle of nerves.

Every bit of her lit up like a firecracker going off. The sensation started in her sex as her muscles clutched his cock tight. The rhythmic waves of pleasure rippled through all her limbs, and stars formed before her eyes.

Daniel thrust one last time and froze, their hips locked together, his cock jerking within her sex. The pulses inside her continued, and he hummed with delight, rocking with his still-rigid cock, extending the bliss until she could bear it no longer and begged for him to stop.

The vibration in her ass finally ceased, but her body's

reactions continued. He pulled from her body, slowly withdrew the toy from her butt—all the while sexual pleasure swept over her and fogged her mind.

The next thing she knew, he was washing her with a warm cloth, tenderly kissing her. He wrapped himself around her and nestled them under the quilt.

"Sleep. I've set the alarm and I'll get you home in plenty of time, but damn if I don't need to hold you for a while longer in my arms."

Another kiss landed on her temple, and she spooned back into his warmth with a grateful sigh. His naked chest pressed against her back, his arms cradling her close. Their breathing matched tempo as they relaxed into a near slumber.

Beth's sleep-clouded mind was still alert to register one thing. Daniel was rapidly coming to be much more than simply sex to her. But exactly what that meant for the future, she really didn't know.

Chapter Twelve

Beth leaned into him harder, and he squeezed her shoulders. Sitting next to him on the bench seat of his truck felt fabulous. There was something so intimate about the way his fingers stroked her, twirling the short hairs at the back of her neck.

"You sure it's okay for me to come along?" she asked again.

"Will you stop it already? For the millionth time, I want you to come." His hand slid behind her back and grasped her waist. He wiggled his fingers under her shirt to caress the bare skin, and she squirmed. "Hmm, I want you to come all the time."

A full-fledged shiver rocked her. "Bad boy. Damn, did you take lessons on how to talk sexy somewhere?"

Daniel continued to stroke her skin as he pulled into the parking lot at the bar. "I come by it naturally. You should hear my dad when he gets going. My mama still blushes like a teenager when he's around."

Beth laughed.

"Besides, Jaxi asked specifically if you would be there. She said she was hoping to get to know you a little better. Travis and Matt said they would come, plus a few of our cousins and friends. Just a chance to catch up now that Jaxi and Blake are back from their honeymoon."

"The twins can't make it?"

"No, they're staying at the college this weekend. They usually only come home for holidays."

Daniel twisted in his seat to kiss her. Cupping her face in his hands, he joined their mouths together for a long, slow, sweet kiss that made her knees weak and her panties wet. She dug her fingers into his hair and kissed him back, getting lost in the taste of him, the sensation of slow drags of his tongue against hers. When his hand left her cheek, she barely noticed until his palm curled around her breast, and it felt so damn good she was ready to crawl into his lap and mount him. Instead, she settled for savouring every stroke. She'd never known that kissing could get her so excited. She felt like one of her teenage students, starry eyed and romanticizing over a crush. Her body warmed under his attention, and she let out a purr of satisfaction.

"Hey, break it up in there, you two. You're fogging the windows."

Beth jerked her lips from Daniel's to stare outside. Or she would have stared out if she could.

"Shit, he's right." Daniel swiped a hand through the moisture clouding the driver's window to reveal Matt's grinning face. "Move your ass or you'll have my door in your ugly mug." He lowered his voice as he turned toward Beth again. "You're mighty distracting, darling."

"I could say the same thing of you."

They smiled at each other.

"You ready for this?"

Beth paused before answering. "It feels as if I'm walking in blind and everyone's going to be staring at me."

"Hmm, don't worry. It's not you but me they're going to look at."

She frowned. "Why?"

He brushed a finger over her lips tenderly. "They're all going to wonder what the hell I did to deserve to be with a knockout like you."

"Ooh, you're smooth, Daniel Coleman, you're smooth."

She could do this. Hell, they'd been in public together for months. Only this was the first night she'd thought of it as them being *together*.

Why did it make such a difference?

He led her into the bar, friendly voices calling their names as they slowly made their way to the back of the room.

"You planning on shooting pool tonight with us?" he asked, waving at yet another group that called his name.

Beth leaned her head toward him. "Is it a guy-territory thing, or am I allowed to trespass, because I'd love to play. We had a table at home when I was growing up."

Daniel pulled her to a halt. "You mention that to my brothers yet? That you can play?"

She shrugged. "Not something that's ever come up in conversation."

Daniel nuzzled her neck and whispered in her ear, "Anyone makes a bet, you take it, okay? I'll spot you the money, but I can see some sweet possibilities for getting even with Matt. He's been gloating about having no competition since the twins went off to college."

The pub was loud with the echoes of laughter and conversation, the music of the dance hall pounding against the far wall and only softly piped into the pool-hall side of the building. Beth glanced with approval at the rich dark tones on the walls, the scent of barbecue ribs making her mouth water.

The sound of familiar voices greeted them as they

approached a large round table pulled off to the side of the busy room.

Jaxi was there, the pretty blonde tucked under Blake's big arm. Four couples, a couple of women, and three more men waved hello. Beth recognized most of the group as part of the extended Coleman clan from around town. She'd been introduced to some of them before, during outings with Daniel.

Matt rose from his chair and came over, hand extended.

"Now that you managed to drag yourselves into public, welcome to our Friday night get-together. Jaxi isn't drinking anything stronger than root beer because of the baby, but we've got draft. Or if you want something else, I'll grab it for you." He gestured to the table where there were pitchers of beer waiting. Beth wrinkled her nose.

"Could I get a rum and Coke? Not much of beer drinker. Sorry."

"No problem. Helen doesn't like beer either. By the way, I'm sorry she's not here to meet you. She had to cancel last minute—some emergency at work."

"Seems she's been working a lot lately," Blake grumbled.

Matt hesitated, his smile twisting for a moment before he turned to Beth. "I'll be right back with your drink."

Jaxi waited until Matt had stepped away from the table before she punched Blake's arm. "Stop poking. It's not his fault Helen's been jamming out on family events."

"Something's up. I wish he'd..." He stopped in mid-grumble, then smiled up at Beth. "And now I'll shut up and be quiet as ordered. Come and join us. We won't bite."

The momentary flash into family politics somehow made her feel more welcome than if everything had been perfect. Beth glanced around the table, counting heads. "I thought Travis was supposed to be here as well."

Jaxi laughed and jerked her thumb over her shoulder to the back of the room. "He's here. He's...busy."

It only took a second to spot what Jaxi indicated. Beth gaped in surprise. "Holy shit."

Travis had a girl pinned against the wall, their hands all over each other. Beth felt embarrassment flush her face, maybe a touch of guilt at the rush she got from being a voyeur. Travis had a double dose of the Coleman good looks, and even with Daniel at her side, Beth could appreciate a nice bit of eye candy.

Although she didn't think it was legal to do in public what they were doing.

"Yeah, 'holy shit' just about covers it." Jaxi kissed Blake's cheek then sat up straighter, patting the seat next to her. "Come and be my buddy. It's good to have another woman hanging out with the Coleman crew. The girls have been sorely outnumbered for the longest time."

Daniel snorted. "Travis's woman doesn't count?"

Jaxi waved a hand. "His most recent flavour of the month? Hello, we don't find out their names half the time. Nor the twins. I've never seen any of those boys with the same woman for more than thirty days."

They did a little wiggling to rearrange chairs, and Beth settled next to the younger woman. The few times they'd done things together, Beth had found her easy to talk with, in spite of their eight-year age difference. Jaxi made her laugh.

"Flavour of the month?"

Jaxi twisted to check out Travis again and slapped a hand over her mouth. "Shoot. Or flavour of the week like this time."

Beth was in the middle of turning to see what Jaxi was

talking about when the woman with the flaming-red miniskirt who had been lip-locked with Travis only moments earlier swished past their table. Her chin stuck out as she headed for the door. With every twitch of the hips, the bare length of her legs flashed.

"Hope she's got blankets in her car for if she gets stuck in a snowbank. Those shoes would be about as useful as spit outside right now." The disdain in Blake's deep voice rang clear.

"Hush, she's trying to look hot." Jaxi wiggled against his side.

"Hmm." He grunted. "Not working. She should try a pair of cowboy boots. Or maybe less war paint."

"Now, Blake, the ladies can't all be the same." Travis sauntered up and folded himself into a chair. A bright red palm print decorated his cheek. He leaned back and stretched his limbs in front of him.

"Damn it, Travis, you're a right bastard sometimes," Blake muttered. "But I'm glad you came out tonight with us."

Travis's cocky smile shifted to something warmer. Almost like he was pleased with Blake's attention.

Beth watched the family dynamics with amusement as the boys proceeded to give Travis hell. There was something about the younger man that seemed a little on the dangerous side, and she was happy when Daniel casually draped his arm around the back of her chair.

Travis raised a brow and whistled softly. "So, the mighty have fallen, have they?"

"Shut up, you ass." Daniel threw a coaster at his brother, but Travis just smirked in response. Daniel tilted his head toward the door. "You've managed to piss off almost every female within a two-hundred-kilometre radius. What happened this time?"

Travis lifted his hands innocently. "Hell if I know. She wanted me to join her somewhere next Friday, and I said I'd already made plans."

"She slapped you for that?" Beth asked in confusion.

Jaxi poked Beth in the side. "Travis is probably forgetting a key phrase or two, right?"

Travis broke out his wicked grin and shrugged. "What? It's not like I told her I had plans to go dancing with Ms. Sylvan Lake or something. Just wanted to hang out with the guys."

"You're such a dog," Matt said. He shook his finger at his younger brother. "You're lucky we don't convince Dad to make you head into Red Deer on deliveries more often, just to mess with your free time."

Travis sat up straight, all trace of his devil-may-care attitude gone. "Speaking of which, I need help. There's a rush order of furniture that I kinda accepted and while we've got everything we need..." He glanced at Daniel sheepishly.

Daniel shook his head. "You didn't. Damn it, Travis, you know we don't mind helping, but could you try to not make it a last-minute emergency every time you notice the sky is falling?"

"I hate the workshop." Travis refilled his mug and leaned back.

Blake echoed his agreement. "It's not my favourite thing either, but it's a part of the family business. There's a lot less fieldwork now that the snow is down, so it makes sense to have something else to do to keep money coming in."

Beside her Daniel tensed for a moment, as if he was about to speak, then sighed softly. She leaned against him and whispered in his ear, "You okay?"

He snuggled her tight to his side and kissed her temple. "Just something I've been thinking about. No firm answers yet, but I might need to borrow your math skills to see if what I'm pondering will work."

The idea of being able to help him, in some area outside the bedroom, made her warm inside.

Matt rubbed his hands together eagerly. "Okay, now that you're all loosened up a bit, who's on the chopping block for pool?"

Travis stood. "I'm in. All that money I saved on drinks tonight is fighting to be free."

"I'm in as well." Daniel turned to her. "Beth, you joining us?"

She followed his lead and went for casual. "Sure. I think I know how." He squeezed her hand under the table, and she fought back her laughter. To hide it, she turned to Jaxi. "Sorry, I'm not being a very good backup girlfriend if I desert you. You want to play?"

Blake growled, and the other boys laughed while Beth stared at Daniel in confusion.

"I'll explain later," he whispered.

Jaxi smirked as she leaned back against her husband, patting the soft rounding barely showing in her belly. "Nah, me and Blake will sit here and argue about names for princess for a while."

Blake choked on his beer. "Don't start on me again."

"Why, Blake, I'm just suggesting you should be ready for anything, maybe even six daughters. That would be so righteous." Jaxi winked at Beth and motioned her away.

Daniel held her hand as they walked to the side of the pool table. "Don't mind them. Jaxi likes to keep Blake off balance."

Beth grinned back. "I think her methodology is excellent." His fingers were warm around hers, and she glanced to see if anyone was watching before sneaking in to kiss him, a fleeting touch on the lips. He tasted good. Daniel pressed a big hand to the middle of her back, holding her against his chest until she'd given him a proper kiss. When she pulled away, he stared back, his gaze tracing her mouth, her eyes. His pupils were dark and growing wider.

"I'm looking forward to taking you home tonight, just so you know."

Beth licked her lips, and he groaned before turning away to grab her a pool cue. Oh damn, the things this man did to her, body and mind and soul.

An hour later Beth dropped the final ball into the pocket, again, and held in her laughter as Matt swore.

"Daniel never warned us you were a shark." He slapped a bill on the edge of the table, and Beth waved it off.

"We're playing for fun. You can keep your money."

Travis grabbed the twenty and stepped closer. "This is part of what makes it fun. People don't beat Matt very often, and it's about damn time. Go ahead, take the cash." He reached around her to slip the money in her back pocket and icy fingers slid up her spine.

She was in his arms, his hands resting lightly on the waistline of her jeans. He grinned saucily, and understanding rolled over her. The ass was testing to see her reaction.

"You lose something, Travis? Or you waiting for me to make sure your next girlfriend likes men who sing soprano?"

Matt snorted and poked Travis in the arm. "Leave her alone, jerk, Daniel doesn't share."

Travis ran his gaze down her body and sighed as he

stepped back to a polite distance. "True. Pity, that."

"You boys are something else." Beth crossed her arms in front of her. "How you've not all ended up on *Wanted* posters all over the country is beyond me."

Travis winked. "Who says we haven't?"

"Where the hell did Daniel get to?" Matt glanced around the bar.

"Fuck." Travis tugged Beth's arm and pulled her toward the pool table, refusing to let her follow the direction of their stares. He turned his bright smile on her and motioned to the table. "How about one final game? Double or nothing?"

"Travis, what's your problem? Let go." She pulled free and found herself blocked by Matt's muscular frame.

He spoke calmly, as if he were dealing with a skittish animal. "Now don't go getting the wrong idea."

She frowned. *What was happening?*

"What kind of wrong idea could I get?" Travis glanced at Matt and the two of them fidgeted, like her boys did when they got caught doing something wrong. "Stop it, both of you, I'm not twelve years old." She shrugged off his hand and poked her head around Travis's big shoulder. "Oh."

Daniel was at the other end of the room, close to the bar counter, clutching their drink refills in either hand. A dark-haired woman stood far too close, pinning him in place. As Beth watched, the woman flung her hands around his neck and locked her lips on his as if she were giving emergency resuscitation. A funny sensation tickled Beth's belly, and she stepped back, considering carefully.

Before tonight they'd made no formal announcement in public that they were a couple, not really. They'd mentioned they were dating to the kids, but no one else. She had no right to be upset, but from a logical, analytical point of view—some hussy was crawling over her man. Time for a decision, that's for sure. In fact it was past time.

"Beth, you okay?"

She turned and lifted a brow at Matt. He and Travis watched her with concern written all over their faces.

"Just fine." She took the couple of steps back to drop into the seat next to Jaxi. This was one of those moments she wanted a female touch. "Who's the woman with a death-wish sucking face with my guy?"

Jaxi snorted behind her hand. "Daniel's ex, Sierra. She dumped him last spring. You want me to come help deal with her?"

Beth stopped to consider. This wasn't Daniel doing something deliberately to hurt her. In fact, when she evaluated what she knew of his character, he would expect her to speak if she wasn't happy.

Standing up for herself was slowly getting easier.

She took a deep breath. "He doesn't want her anymore, does he?"

"Hell, no. I'm surprised to even see her here. We've all made it pretty clear she's not welcome in our circle. She turned out to be a self-centered bitch, if you'll excuse me for saying it."

Beth sighed. "Thanks. Okay, I think I can handle one hormonally challenged, poorly groomed woman."

Blake choked again and Jaxi patted his back. "Don't worry, dear, it's a girl thing. Like you'll have to deal with our daughters down the road."

By the time she rose and made her way to where Daniel stood attempting to untangle himself from the woman's clutches, Beth was still undecided what tack to take. It was obvious Daniel wasn't the instigator, but he needed to learn there was a time to stop being such a gentleman.

She reached his side shortly after Sierra finally let loose the vacuum seal on a second kiss and Daniel tried to get a word in edgewise. The creature covered his mouth with her hand and pouted prettily.

"I've missed you so much," she said in a husky voice.

Beth fought to keep from retching. The dramatic effect the woman was attempting was so pathetic.

"There you are, sweetheart, can I get that for you?" Beth carefully took one of the glasses from Daniel's fingers and smiled at him. Finally able to move, Daniel stepped clear of the clutches of his ex. He wiped at his mouth with the back of his hand and grimaced.

"Beth, you want to meet Sierra before she leaves?"

Beth raised a brow and looked the woman up and down slowly. Okay, the ex-girlfriend was good looking, but damn it, Daniel was hers now. Sierra had missed her chance.

"Not really. Not unless she wants to explain why she was clinging to my lover like a piece of Saran Wrap?"

"Lover?" Sierra sputtered. She glared at Daniel. "But you... But we..."

"Split up. A long time ago now, and that's the end of it."

"But, I thought maybe we could try again."

Beth sighed. Sierra was obviously not one of the brighter bulbs in the room. There was no need to be unpleasant about it. As long as the woman didn't even *think* of making another move.

Daniel wrapped an arm around Beth's waist as he shook his head. "You thought wrong. Beth and I are seeing each other, and if you don't mind, we'll be returning to our friends."

The woman stared in silence as they walked away. Halfway back to the table, Beth glanced up to discover everyone was watching, their eyes glued to the drama. Travis and Blake wore matching smirks, Matt looked impressed. Jaxi pumped a fist in the air in victory. Yeah, there was a place for her in their midst, and she felt surprisingly comfortable with that. But the fact she hadn't even known Daniel had an ex in town bothered her. A lot. Heck, she'd never imagined he was a monk before he met her. Suddenly she wanted to know it all. Who he had dated, what he had loved to do while growing up. What his dreams were for the future.

Holy cow, somewhere in the past two minutes she'd realized she really cared about the big cowboy. She almost felt she should run after Sierra and shake her hand enthusiastically for pushing the right buttons.

Beth was falling in love, and the thought didn't make her sick to her stomach.

She tugged his hand and led him to the side of the room, staring up at him seriously for a minute.

Daniel touched her check gently. "I'm sorry about that. I had no idea she was going to be here, and then I couldn't figure out how to get away without—"

She pressed her fingers over his lips. Yeah, he should have cut the woman off a lot faster, but his tender heart was part of what she appreciated about him. Time to jump in with two feet and stop holding back.

"You know, we've spent an awful lot of time together in the past months, and it appears we haven't talked about anything more important than the weather and where our next sexual tryst is going to be."

He frowned. "We've mentioned a few things but...you're right. I was thinking that the other day as well."

"It's not easy, not with the kids around. And I know I haven't been the best at opening up. I'm going to work on changing that, okay?"

There was a flash of delight in his eyes. "You're not mad at me for that little display with Sierra?"

She shook her head. "Not your fault. Only, if a woman does an octopus imitation on you again, you are allowed to *accidentally* pour the drinks in your hands on her. That would make her let go quick enough."

He chuckled. "Yes, ma'am, I'll remember that."

She wrapped her arms around him and rested her head on his chest. The scent of Sierra's perfume hit her, and she wrinkled her nose.

"Ugh. You smell like that woman." Daniel laughed as he leaned over to kiss her. She pressed her hands against him and turned her face away. "No sir. You're sterilizing those lips before I kiss you again."

He tucked her fingers into the crook of his arm to lead her back to their table. Somehow in the next while they would find the time and ways to start sharing with each other.

Beth took her seat at Daniel's side, surrounded by the Coleman clan. Maybe making a few more friends along the way would be a good idea was well.

Chapter Thirteen

Gabe jotted down a few final ideas before closing his notebook. "That was exactly what I needed to know. Thanks, Allison. I'm glad I spotted your name when I went researching. The government information online was plain enough, but getting to talk to someone actually in the business makes it seem more real. I'm going to have to think a bit how we'll be able to follow up."

His dining mate, an old classmate from high school who now lived and worked in Red Deer, raised her water glass and smiled. "I hope you decide it's worth your while. There's a call for quality organic meat, and I'm more than happy to use local growers for the restaurants we service. The demand is definitely higher than the supply."

"Your website mentioned that. About wanting to use local suppliers when possible. That's part of what made me contact you in the first place." The fact Allison was a beautiful woman who he already had connections with didn't hurt matters either, but this was business. No way was Gabe willing to mess up something that could be the savior of their financial future for a tumble. No matter how attractive she'd turned out. The years she'd been gone had been good to her. "I like the idea you're still working in the community, in a new way. I appreciate that."

Allison shared a wide smile with him, his compliment obviously making her happy. "Are you staying in Red Deer tonight?" she asked.

Gabe shook his head. "Back home this afternoon. My brother picked up the slack today, but I can't be gone too long."

"Do you have time for a tour of our shop? There're a few classes and weekend workshops I have information on that might help. I forgot to bring the brochures along, but if now isn't good, I can email you the links instead."

Someone upstairs liked him. "I have time. Thanks for offering. Thank you for everything."

Allison accepted his outstretched hand and shook it firmly. "Always glad to see a familiar face from my hometown, and hey, if this works out, I'll be in a winning situation as well. If you give me a minute, I'll meet you at the door and you can follow me over."

Gabe rose to his feet and pulled out her chair, caving far enough to allow himself to watch her hips in admiration as he followed her to the front. He took care of the bill and waited for her to return.

His reflection in the window behind the cash register displayed his enormous foolish grin. He couldn't help it—the delight filling him at actually having come this far? Man, it felt good.

He'd come up with an idea, and it wasn't even a halfcocked idea at that. All the requirements Allison had listed to become a registered organic beef farm were possible on the land his family owned. The idea was radical—a complete departure from the way his father ran the spread, but the end result?

It might be enough. The attempt would certainly be interesting.

A familiar laugh carried to his ears, interrupting his mental calculations, and he glanced back into the restaurant. The place was bright with midday sun, and it wasn't hard to spot the source. Understanding what he saw was more difficult. Helen Meridan leaned forward over one of the tiny tables at the far edge of the room, an older man seated across from her holding her fingers in his.

Gabe stared, waiting for her to pull back. Waiting for a sign this was a business handshake—like the one he'd just given to Allison that had been all above board and legit.

He waited, hoping what he suspected wasn't really happening, because right now it looked an awful lot like his cousin Matt's steady girlfriend was holding hands with a stranger.

He wasn't in the know about everything going on in his cousin's life, or Helen's, but he was damn sure she didn't have a reason to be hours away from Rocky with another man. Especially one old enough to—no, he refused to even conjecture. But when the man raised her hand to his lips and kissed her knuckles, Gabe's mouth turned sour.

Fuck it.

He must have spoken the words, must have cussed far louder than he intended. Helen's head swiveled and her eyes went wide. She turned briefly back to her seatmate and pulled her hand free, rose and made her way over to where Gabe stood, feeling slightly slack-jawed. The man at the table stared after her, a small frown building as if he was shocked at Helen's rapid departure.

She brushed past Gabe and pulled him with her to the edge of the hall that led to the bathrooms. By the time she turned to face him, her face was covered by a bright smile.

"Hey, you. Didn't expect to see you this far from home."

He bet she didn't. "Helen, what the hell is going on?"

She bit her lower lip and glanced toward the ceiling. The sick sensation in his stomach grew every second she hesitated.

He'd seen this woman in a stressful situation before—a stressful sexual situation to be exact. While he didn't expect having been invited by Matt into her bed for a temporarily ménage gave any lasting privileges, it sure the hell made Gabe more responsible than he would have been otherwise.

Helen grabbed the front of his shirt and pulled his ear closer to her mouth. "Fine. I didn't want anyone to know, so you've got to keep it a secret. It's a job interview."

For fuck's sake. "For what? Becoming a call girl?"

Helen jerked back, shock in her expression. "A call... What are you talking about?"

"He was kissing you, Helen. I ain't never had an interview where I kissed anything but ass, figuratively, that one time I really needed some cash."

"The kiss? *Jesus*, Gabe." She waved him off. "He's old-fashioned, that's all. It's his style. He kissed the waitress's hand when we were seated. You want to go and give her the third degree as well? Maybe he's starting a brothel or something."

Gabe hesitated for a moment. She glared back, indignation written all over her. Only, he could have sworn a moment ago he'd seen her confused and panicked.

Helen dragged a hand through her hair. "Look, it's just an interview, but...I haven't said anything to Matt yet because I'm not sure anything is going to come of it. Can you keep it quiet for a while? I should know within a couple weeks."

Another jolt of unease hit. Keeping that kind of secret didn't sit well.

He hadn't even had time to respond before she smiled and poked him in the chest. "So what are you doing here? You never get this far out of Rocky anymore."

With one swoop, his tongue was frozen. Like hell would he

mention anything about his ideas for changing his family's ranch before they were even half-baked. Especially not to Helen, who shared others' information as rapidly as a flag shook in a brisk wind. His father was going to be hellishly difficult to deal with anyway. A heads-up warning could ruin everything.

To top off his shitty dilemma, Allison appeared from the ladies' room and was rapidly approaching behind Helen's back. Gabe's mind raced—what could he say to cover his tracks? Helen knew Allison from school as well.

His luck had run out.

"I'm on a date." He was screwed. Please, God, let Allison forgive him. He ducked past Helen and reached for Allison. She frowned slightly but accepted his hand. One tug allowed him to move in close. He planted his mouth by her ear as he wrapped his arms around her in a pseudo-lover's clutch. "Sorry, I need your help. Play along, please..."

He twisted them, keeping Allison under his arm. "Babe, you remember Helen?"

Allison stood at his side, a trifle on the stiff side. Then, glory be, she passed her arm behind his back, around his hip and slipped her fingers into his belt loop. It was as if she melted in, all cozy and soft, and for a split second Gabe was very sad this was only a ploy.

"Helen. Haven't seen you in forever." Allison spoke politely but without much invitation in her tone.

Helen said hello, her gaze jumping back and forth between them. Then she seemed to lose all interest and shrugged. "Hey, don't mean to be rude, but I need to get back to the table. Nice to see you, Allison. Gabe..."

She stared for a second, an implied finger-to-the-lips there before she turned her back and strolled casually toward the seating area.

Gabe's heart rate hovered well above normal, but now he wasn't sure if it was from dodging a bullet or from the sweet scent of Allison in his arms.

He released her, and they separated, heading though the door in silence. They were well into the parking lot before she glanced back, then burst out laughing. "Gabriel Coleman, it seems some things never change. What was that all about? You trying to make her jealous or—?"

"God, no. Exactly the opposite."

She laughed harder. "Sorry, but the idea one of the Angel Boy Colemans just used me to avoid a woman makes me a little giddy."

Gabe's cheeks heated. Screw it, she was making him blush. "Hate that bloody nickname with a vengeance—it's worse than what my Six Pack cousins have to put up with. Look, I'm sorry, but I didn't want to have to explain what we were doing together. It's none of her business."

"Well, that's true, and seeing you with a woman on a...*date*...is probably totally un-newsworthy."

He sighed. "That's one of those 'damned if I do, damned if I don't' statements."

Allison's laugh was downright addictive, and he considered again why he'd never gone out with her when they were in high school. "Yeah, I promise not to make you answer. Forget it, no harm done. Come on, I'll show you the shop."

Gabe waited until she'd gotten into her car before he headed to his truck, marveling how this fact-finding excursion had gotten so complicated. Wondering how crazy it was to be thinking about Allison when he had a life to change a hundred kilometers away from her.

Chapter Fourteen

Beth tossed a few more pillows on the couch and pointed firmly. "Sit."

Jaxi opened her mouth to protest then slammed it shut, lowering herself and curling her legs up. "You know, it's not often I agree to this kind of nonsense."

"Nonsense?" Karen Coleman shoved a potato chip into her mouth. "You mean abandoning the guys, ordering a pizza and putting your feet up while you do nothing for an entire evening?"

Jaxi grinned sheepishly. "I will admit getting pizza brought in is a treat and a half. But it feels weird to leave Blake for the night, if that doesn't sound all little wimpy girlish. I like spending time with him, even if we are married and all."

Karen laughed. "I hope you're still enjoying his company. You worked hard enough to catch the man."

"Damn right, I did." Jaxi raised her glass of juice. "So, what do you want to gossip about then? Who's got a hot new beau they want to share about? Although, Beth, you can't share anything because hearing you talk about Daniel and sex would be way too weird."

"So this isn't a pre-pre-baby shower?" Beth teased.

Jaxi snorted. "Hell no. I'm only in my first trimester. I hope I'm not really showing for a good long time, because you know it's going to get impossible when my belly is big enough the Coleman boys remember every second of every day. I won't be able to move, they'll try to wrap me so tight in cotton."

"You'll get enough real baby showers from the rest of everyone down the road. Tonight is just a break—anything the pregnant mom-to-be wants."

"Pickles and ice cream?" Karen's sister Tamara poked her head out of the kitchen, pushing the door open with her shoulders and bringing in a tray covered with goodies.

"Don't be trite. That's so stereotypical." Karen removed a few items from the table and helped balance the load on the way down. "Hmmm, but chocolate chip cookies are good even if you're not preggers."

Beth smiled at the small group of women gathered in Tamara's apartment. "Sometimes the stereotypes are true, sorry to say. I had cravings with every one of my kids."

The conversation took off, and Beth leaned back happily on the couch, diving into the chips and dip and enjoying some female companionship. The knock on the door came far sooner than any of them expected. Beth glanced at her watch in surprise.

She opened the door to discover Daniel's red-cheeked smile. "Is it really that time already?"

"It's late, and you said you were going to turn into a pumpkin if you didn't get to bed on schedule." He slipped into the room and pulled off his toque and gloves. "Ladies. I'm the taxi service for the night. I have to steal away two of your party, if you don't mind."

Karen threw popcorn at him. "Spoilsport."

"Saucy thing. Hey, you going to stop by and help clear the ice for the skating party before Christmas or should I tell my dad not to bother?"

"What? No ice? That would be anti-holiday. That's like announcing no toboggan party on Boxing Day. You being the Grinch or something?" Tamara handed over a paper bag and Daniel frowned. She grinned. "Leftover pizza. Don't ever say the Whiskey Creek Colemans don't take care of you better than you deserve."

Jaxi shrugged on her coat and boots, and Beth joined her, bundling against the cold. She turned to give both Karen and Tamara big hugs. "Thanks, girls, that was just what I needed. And anytime you want to come over, you let me know."

Daniel led them to his truck, and Beth ended up hip to hip at his side, hot air blowing hard over the three of them as they shared the bench seat. "That was a lot of fun. Thanks for inviting me, Jaxi."

Jaxi leaned back, head resting on the window. "Yup, no problem. The girls are sweet, and I love doing stuff with them. Hopefully they'll be able to stay in the area."

"Why would they leave?"

Daniel answered first. "Tamara's got her nursing degree and the apartment in town, but Karen and their little sister Lisa are interested in working the land. It isn't easy to convince their dad that they can deal with doing 'a man's job'." He shrugged, his hands firm on the wheel as he took them back over the slippery roads. "I don't agree with Uncle George, especially since Karen is one of the best horse women I've ever seen. But...tradition."

Jaxi's eyes were closed. "Tradition sucks."

"I'm not arguing with you, Jaxi. Just telling how it is."

Beth rested her hand on Daniel's thigh and let his heat warm her fingers. They were all quiet for the rest of the trip, Daniel driving Jaxi right up to the guest cabin. Blake was there immediately, coming from the main house to wrap an arm around her.

"I'm hitting the sack—this being pregnant is wiping me out. Night, Beth. Daniel, thanks for the ride."

They waved her off and Daniel backed up carefully. "You too tired for a short walk? You're dressed for the weather—I thought we could walk the trail back to the Peter's house—leave my truck here."

Beth smiled. "A walk would clear a few cobwebs before I try to sleep. The babysitter is—"

"Shoot, I forgot about her." He changed route and headed down the main drive and around to her front door. "Change of plans. We'll still go for a walk, but this way I can drive Sandy home, okay?"

Beth took a deep breath of the cold air, the slight tinge of wood smoke from the fireplaces bouncing on her tongue and making her senses come to life. She tucked her glove-covered hand into the crook of his elbow, and they stepped along the well-packed trail. Her boys didn't give fresh snow any time to accumulate without racing through and marking it up with toboggans and miniature snowshoes.

They were nearly halfway around the loop before she realized she hadn't said a word. "Sorry, I'm not being very good company, am I?"

Daniel tugged his arm in closer and squeezed her fingers. "Figured you had something on your mind. I don't need to be filling the air with noise to enjoy your company. But if there's something you want to talk about, I'm here."

Beth stopped to stare over the snow-covered field. The moon shone down, creating a narrow strip of glimmer in the midst of the powdery white. "I had a good time tonight."

Daniel stepped behind and wrapped his strong arms around her, tugging her to his body until she was surrounded.

159

Protected. "Why does that sound as if you're trying to convince yourself?"

"No, I did have fun. Just...made me think all kinds of things. Sort of one thought led to another, and my brain is so full right now I'm not sure if I'm coming or going."

He *hmm*ed, but other than that, simply waited.

She was telling the truth. She'd enjoyed the outing—but it stood in such sharp contrast to what her life had been like before, the comparison hurt. The memories ached.

"I haven't had a lot of girlfriends. Getting out for a night alone...rarely happened. I enjoyed myself, and yet the pleasure of it made me sad that I missed time and friendships over the past years."

She tried to say it plain and simple. No blame, because there wasn't a place to put blame anymore.

Daniel turned her to face him. "I can see that. It's almost a teeter-totter, or as if you've been given something and then had it taken away. You didn't know how much you'd miss it because you'd never experienced it."

Beth sighed. "You're a wise man, Daniel."

He shook his head. "Not really. Just, well, it's nothing like what you've dealt with, but I know..."

This time when he paused, Beth was the one to touch his chest and get his attention back from where she'd lost him. "What's going on in your head?"

He spoke slowly. "I don't know that it's the time for that talk. You warm enough?"

"Tons warm." She rested her head on his chest and synchronized her breathing with his. "Daniel, am I a terrible person for being a tiny bit jealous that Jaxi's pregnant?"

He sucked in a quick gasp. If she hadn't been touching him

so intimately, she probably wouldn't have noticed. "I don't think you could do anything that would make you terrible."

Beth clung to her inner fears, refusing to voice them. She might have said they were going to open up more, and she was trying. Even the confession she'd just made was hard enough.

Other secrets were staying buried and dead.

"I am jealous. Just a little bit of me."

"Doesn't make you a terrible person. You got your reasons, and that's facts and life. If you want to know..." He let out a long slow breath. "I understand, maybe not for the same reasons, but I'm a bit jealous myself."

"You are?"

He cupped her face, his glove warming quickly against her skin. "Well, not that I want morning sickness and a big enough belly I can't see my toes, no. Maybe I should have said I'm jealous of my brother, but that could sound as if I wish I'd knocked up Jaxi, and that's not it either."

He was trying to reduce the stress, she understood where his lighthearted words came from. A laugh escaped in spite of the burning inside. "I can't have any more babies."

His smile vanished. "Damn, I'm sorry. I shouldn't have been joking around. I—"

She covered his mouth with her hand. "You didn't know, and I get it. But I wanted you to know. It's awkward, but it's a part of my life. I had a miscarriage after Robbie. It was bad, and I..."

Her throat choked up tight.

He squeezed her again, pushing out the pain and allowing her to hide her face. Or was it for his own sake? She wondered a moment later when he spoke toward her ear, his face buried her neck. "I can't have kids, I mean, not get anyone pregnant.

Caught the mumps last winter and it did a number on my system."

The pain inside intensified, but now it was for his sake, not her own. "God, Daniel. I'm so sorry."

She'd thought there was no way a man could possibly understand—but she'd been wrong. It was there in his touch, the tender way he surrounded her as if guarding her from more harm. Sharing his own hidden hurts, his unanswerable desires. She held his head against her, breathing in the same air. The warmth from his lungs heated it, leaving only a slight bite of the icy weather around them to bring in refreshing cold.

They stood for the longest time. Snow slid off branches, landing with plops beside them. Beth sighed then leaned back even as his arms held her cradled against his body.

For today, she thought they'd both had enough sharing. "Well, that was a shining way to end the day."

He laughed, a low rumble filled with sympathy and caring. "Oh, Miss Beth. Don't you apologize for letting me in on one of your secrets. One of your precious memories and hurts. I'm so honoured right now you trusted me."

Trust. It was coming. "Me too. Thank you for letting me know."

Daniel stroked a finger down her cheek, brushing away a tear she didn't realize had fallen. "Life goes on."

That truth contained both pain and hope. "It does seem strange to be so happy for someone and still have this ball of hurt wrapped up inside."

"And there's not much a person can say to make it easier. Well-intended platitudes cut like a knife."

She nodded then shivered, unable to stop it from showing.

"That's our signal it's time to head in." He put a hand on

her back, ready to aim her down the path to the house.

"Wait."

He stopped, confusion on his gentle face. She reached up and cupped his cheek, pressing her lips to his and kissing him. Putting her heart behind it. When she pulled away, he didn't say anything, just smiled and guided her home.

Chapter Fifteen

The dishwater swirled down the drain. The constant yattering of the boys as they dried the dishes and wiped the table felt comfortable, and Daniel spotted the silly grin he wore in the hall mirror as he scooped up the littlest one and tickled him en route to the living room.

"Okay, partners, your mama will be home in a couple hours, so let's make sure we've got everything shipshape. Lance, you got the list?"

"We've done it all." He held out the paper and pointed. "Homework, supper, dishes, chores."

"Everything?"

Lance nodded. Robbie squirmed out of his arms and climbed on the couch, bouncing up and down excitedly. "We get to play more games."

Chaos ensued. Beth was due back from her teachers' development field trip by nine. Daniel had been honoured when she asked him if he wanted to step in and take the boys for the day. Her placing that kind of trust in him was humbling and made him feel very hopeful about the future. Yet after a full day with all three tykes, he was ready to admit he was exhausted. "Where do you kids get your energy from?"

They'd played hide and seek outdoors in the snow and the trees. Nathan discovered one of the cats had a new batch of kittens, the family hidden in the far recesses of the barn. Throughout the day, while helping the boys make forts in the bales of the loft and chasing the rest of the barn cats in circles, Daniel had flashbacks to his own childhood. Roaming the countryside with his brothers like a wild creature during the hours of freedom between chores.

Robbie leapt off the couch and tackled him. Then all three boys were on him, wrestling him down and tickling him as he laughed out loud at their antics.

The roughhousing calmed eventually, and Daniel guided them into playing a few final board games. He lit the fire and happily accepted the book Lance passed him. The kid's dark eyes bored into him for a minute, like he was offering a challenge. Daniel glanced at the tome in his hands and chuckled to himself. Another test. Lance seemed to be all about the tests.

"*Farmer Boy*. Awesome story."

Lance frowned. "Mom said we had to read it, but it's a girl's book."

Daniel let his mouth hang open in an exaggerated fashion, playing it up for the kids. "You're joking, right? Haven't you read the rest of the *Little House* books? When we were all kids, my daddy sat us down every Friday evening for reading time, starting with that series."

"Really?"

"Really. They ain't books for just girls. Heck, the experiences that family had were tough and exciting. I know when I heard some of the things they lived through it always made me real grateful for all the comforts of home I got to enjoy. And thankful for treats like ice cream in the freezer instead of only once in a blue moon."

Daniel settled on the couch and started reading at the

bookmark. Robbie nestled against him, and Lance and Nathan plopped on the floor. Every time he glanced over, Lance's thoughtful expression made him wonder what the hell was going on in the kid's head.

Two hours later he finally had them tucked into bed, and a brand-new appreciation for why Beth was often tired when he called her. The phone rang, and he laughed as he spotted the number on the display.

"Evening, darling."

"Hey, Daniel. We're running late, and it's going to be an hour still before I get home. Everything okay?"

He collapsed into the La-Z-Boy chair in front of the fire, kicking the foot extension out and relaxing back with a groan. "Everything's great, but you are getting a massage the next time I see you. How the hell do you do this every day, woman?"

Her sexy voice lowered a notch. "Welcome to my world. Oh, and I'm totally accepting your offer, I need the massage so bad. My feet are killing me. I swear they made us walk every inch of the Tyrrell Museum. I'd sit through a million meetings before going on another 'teachers' field trip'."

"Your leg sore?"

"Amazingly, not too bad. I think all the walks we've been taking have strengthened it." Static cut in on the line and she spoke quickly. "I'll see you at home as soon as I can."

Home. Home with him where she belonged.

He rattled around the house for a bit, now too keyed up to stare into the fire and relax. The past couple of days they'd tried a few times to get together to talk, but it was like the kids had radar and woke up right when the discussion got deeper than sharing growing-up stories. There were certain things neither of them wanted to discuss in a public coffee shop or over the phone. Daniel sighed.

Tonight he intended to ask if Jaxi's offer of babysitting was a possibility. See if Beth was willing to go on a retreat, just the two of them, for a couple of nights. Not only to get to make love without pulling strings, but to talk—really talk.

A creak on the stairs sounded with a low whimper hard on its heels. A little head poked around the corner, Nathan's big eyes staring at him.

"Nathan? What's up, bud?"

"I'm thirsty."

Oh Lord. Daniel got him a glass of water and led the kid into the living room to sit in front of the fire. Of course, this probably meant he'd be up right around the time Beth got home, having to pee.

Kids.

Daniel sat back in the recliner. Moving slow and staying silent. Whenever he'd tried to stay up past his bedtime that was what his daddy had done. Made it seem peaceful and quiet. To a seven-year-old, boring.

Nathan perched on his heels and sipped slowly, his gaze darting around the room and returning again and again to Daniel. There was almost nothing left in the glass and still he milked it. Daniel scratched his face to hide his grin.

"You ready for me to tuck you in again?"

Nathan put the glass down on the coffee table and turned those big eyes on Daniel. "I'm scared to go to bed."

Daniel frowned. Now what was going on? "Something wrong with your room? Did you know that's the room my brother Blake used to sleep in? It's a nice big space, and you've got Robbie in there to keep you company."

"Not that." The tyke surprised him to pieces by crawling into his lap and tugging on his shirt. "Bad dreams."

Ahh. "Like there's something..." *Maybe giving the kid ideas wasn't the best way to go about this.* "What kind of dreams?"

"Of my daddy."

Fuck. For all the time they'd spent together, it had shocked him how seldom the kids ever mentioned their father. Hell, at their age his daddy had been the center of his universe, and every waking minute he'd been home from school he'd tagged along, trying to keep up. Looking back he probably got in the way more than he helped, but Mike had never said a word.

"You miss him?"

Nathan stiffened in his lap. He swung his head up and glared at Daniel. "Can I ask you something?"

"Shoot."

"You ever hit someone? Like punch them and hurt them?"

Daniel chuckled. "I've got five brothers. You tell me, you ever scuffle with Robbie or Lance?"

Nathan's face folded into a frown. "Well, that's different. They deserve it."

"I expect they do, sometimes. I know my brothers certainly do."

"You ever hit a girl?"

"Hell no. I don't have any sisters, but I still can't imagine hitting one." The memory of Sierra planting the kiss on him in the bar crossed his mind. "They can be very annoying creatures at times, girls, but I'd never hit one."

"What if a girl asks for it?"

Daniel frowned. What the hell kinda question was that from a seven-year-old? "You mean like teasing you? You still need to treat them nice, even if they call you names. Even if they poke you." He leaned over and lowered his voice. "I know at times it just don't seem fair, but if you can learn it now, it'll make things a whole lot better when you get older."

"Daddy said Mommy asked for it."

His breath was sucked from his lungs as Nathan's thin voice carried through the night air. Daniel held in the swear words wanting to escape. He'd wondered if her husband had abused her. He's suspected that was part of the secret Beth had kept, and yet the absolute fury that rose in his belly was shocking.

Holy shit, now what could he say? "All I can tell you is what I've been taught. There ain't nothing a girl can do that makes it right for you to hit her. That doesn't mean you have to stand there and take it, your mama has strong opinions on letting anyone push you around, but hitting them back? No sir. That's not what a gentleman does."

Nathan snuggled in tighter to Daniel's side and something twisted in his belly. The earthy scent of boy, familiar and yet strange, rose to his nose. He tentatively put an arm around the little tyke and gave him a squeeze.

"I didn't like it when he hit Mommy."

Another shot of pain streaked through Daniel. "Of course you didn't."

"I wanted to hit him." Nathan's voice was so soft and low, Daniel barely heard the words. Red-hot anger at the man he didn't even know blazed out. If the bastard hadn't already been dead, Daniel would have happily tracked him down and shot him.

Daniel rocked the boy, considering his words carefully. "Nathan, I ain't going to tell you that you're wrong. In wanting to defend your mama, you were completely right. Now I didn't know your daddy, and I don't know all that happened along the way, but I can tell you this. Taking care of our mamas and sisters, and women in general, is supposed to be important to every man."

He lifted Nathan's face to look directly into his tear-filled eyes. "That what you having bad dreams about? Your daddy hitting your mama?" Nathan's chin quivered. "Shit."

Nathan's eyes grew wide. "You swore. Mama says we're not supposed to swear."

Daniel put his finger over his lips for a second. "You're right, and I try not to, but there's just some times it sneaks out. Like when I'm really mad."

The kid snorted. "You're not mad."

"Oh yes, I am. Not at you, but for you."

Nathan frowned. "But you're not yelling or throwing things. You can't be mad."

Oh my Lord, give me the words. Daniel pressed his hand to Nathan's head and drew him up against his chest.

"Trust me, I'm real mad." How the hell was he supposed to explain to the kid that what he'd experienced should never have happened? "There're a few kinds of anger in the world. There's the throwing things kind of mad—that doesn't really get much done except hurt the things you throw and the people you throw them at, does it?"

"Hurts them lots." Nathan's voice shook.

Sweet Jesus. The whole conversation made his mind and heart ache. What kind of bastard could do this to his own children? To his wife? "Then there's the kind of mad that makes people want to make things better. That's the kind of mad I am. I'm upset for you and your brothers. I'm angry for your mama's sake, but yelling and throwing things would only make it worse."

Nathan nodded rapidly.

There was no way he could continue this conversation

tonight. "You just relax right here. I'll keep the bad dreams away. Deal?"

Nathan sniffed and wiped at his nose, then cocooned in like one of the kittens under their mom out in the barn. It took a couple of minutes for his breathing to relax from the rasping little gasps it had become as he'd fought back tears.

The room quieted. The fire crackled softly, the chair squeaked on every rock. Above their heads the floorboards of the old house expanded and contracted. The snow slid off one section of the roof from the heat of the fire. Daniel leaned his head back and tried to sort out all the emotions racing through him.

Beth's husband had abused her. Emotionally abused the kids too from what Nathan had let slip. They seemed to be dealing with it well, and his admiration for Beth increased astronomically.

She was strong, desirable, and damn if he was going to let her hide away from him anymore.

The time of waiting became like a time of prayer. He mentally listed all the things he was grateful for, all the things he wanted. And the longer he sat, with a child in his arms, waiting for his woman to return, the more he realized everything he still wanted was nearly within his grasp.

If Beth was ready to trust him with her heart.

The deck boards outside the door creaked a moment before Beth stepped inside. She came into the living room, sparkling snow crystals in her hair and her cheeks rosy from the cold. Daniel could have stared at her all night long.

"Hey, what's up?" she whispered as she knelt beside the chair, one hand resting on his arm, the other reaching to brush the hair from Nathan's face.

"He's okay. I just didn't want to take him upstairs in case

we woke up Robbie and you weren't home yet. He had a bad dream."

"He has them occasionally." She stared at her son for a moment, and written on her face was such sadness and loss he couldn't take it anymore.

"Beth, we need to talk."

She nodded slowly, her fingers fidgeting with the fabric of his sleeve. "Let's tuck him in."

They went upstairs together, and Daniel stepped back after carefully placing the now boneless Nathan on his bed. Standing in the doorway, he watched Beth tenderly pulled up the covers and kiss both Nathan and Robbie. Then she slipped past him to check on Lance, closing his curtains and turning off his MP3.

When she would have walked down the stairs, he grabbed her hand and tugged her toward her bedroom. "You must be tired. Come on, I'll give you that massage I promised."

Her breathing picked up as her gaze flickered to the closed doors of the boys.

Daniel lifted her chin in his hand. "Nothing will happen that you don't want to, okay? I promise. If you want me to crawl out the window so you don't get caught with me in your room, I'll do it. I even know which trees I have to climb down to get away safely."

That was enough to bring a smile back to her face, and she laughed softly and pulled him after her, turning the lock. "I've been teaching the boys they are supposed to knock before entering, but they weren't learning very fast. So they're used to me locking the door now."

She pulled off her sweater and stretched her arms in the air. "I never want to go on another field trip in my life."

"Not into dinosaurs?" Daniel sat on the chair in the corner

of the room and watched, mesmerized, as Beth sat on the bed and stripped off her socks and wiggled out of her slacks.

They needed to get to the real issue, but she was tying his brain in knots.

He joined her on the bed, crawling behind her to massage her shoulders, her neck. Pressing his thumbs into the tight muscles until she began to relax under this touch.

"We're not doing a lot of talking, are we?"

Daniel laughed. "Not really sure where to begin."

Beth placed a hand on his where it rested on her shoulder. Then she glanced up at him. "Did Nathan tell you what his bad dream was about?"

He moved in front of her, kneeling at her feet. "He did. Kinda, like a seven-year-old tells any story."

He wrapped his arms around her and hugged her tight to him, just needing to squeeze out some of the hurt and agony he saw in her eyes. Beth sniffed a couple of times and then swore.

"I promised myself I wasn't going to do this anymore."

"Do what?"

"Cry for the no-good bastard. Cry because of him. I want to move on and forget what he did to me and the boys, and yet he's still there, haunting us."

She tucked her tear-streaked face into the crook of his neck, and his heart broke. "You go ahead and cry. You love your sons, and until you know they are on the road to understanding what the real love of family means, you're going to have moments you cry. Hell, my mama still cries over the stupid things her sons do to each other, and she cries when we get our feelings hurt, and we're all grown up. You're a good mama to your boys, Beth, and tears come with the territory."

She leaned back and cupped his face in her hand. "Daniel,

you are one in a million. That's sweet of you, but there are things you don't know. Like if I really loved my boys I should have left the man years ago, before he had a chance to make our life hell. I should have left the first time he hit me, but I was like every one of the women who think they'll be the exception. That he really was sorry for what he'd done. That he really never would do it again. That the boys were better off with a father who was decent most of the time."

Daniel held in his anger. "You shouldn't have had to make the decision. None of it was your fault, Beth."

"Nathan cries because his dad is gone, and you know what, that is my fault. I'm the one who killed him."

He choked back his surprise. "You said he died in the car crash."

"He did."

Daniel waited, stroking her hair gently, giving her the space to tell it her own way.

She wiggled back on the bed and wrapped her arms around herself, voice low, head dipped. "He'd found out something I'd done that he didn't like. I can't even remember what it was, and he was cursing a blue streak at me. The roads were icy that night—I didn't want to drive in the first place, but he insisted—and when I felt myself losing control of the vehicle I..." she paused, "...I yanked the wheel to the side and we spun into traffic with the passenger side leading. I made sure he was the one in the direct line of anything that hit us."

Hell, had she really taken on that burden? "Beth, if you were already skidding, there's no way anything you did changed which direction the car turned."

Her head snapped up, a flicker of something in her eyes that could have been hope, but it vanished too quickly for him to be sure.

"Still, it was a conscious choice. I'd do it again in an instant." She was breathing so fast he thought she might faint. "I can't believe I'm telling you this, but I need to explain—"

He hurried to reassure her. "You don't have to explain anything more to me. Not right now. I want to know, but only when you're ready to talk about it. Not because you think I'm expecting you to." He held her hands clasped in his, aching to help her, wanting to comfort her. Her fingers were icy cold, and he warmed them gently in his palms. "I still think you can forgive yourself for his death. I'm sure there was an investigation, and if you had done anything wrong, they would have discovered it then. It was an accident—that's all it was."

"I was happy he was dead, though. He was a bastard. Stole away years of my life. Made the boys quake in fear. Made me have sex when he knew it was dangerous. Demanded I keep going until..."

She stopped. Completely. His heart was breaking for her, for every bit of pain she'd suffered.

"Until what? Oh God, Beth."

She whipped her head around, hair flying. Her eyes were dark, not with the heat of passion he was used to seeing but with pure unadulterated rage.

"My baby girl died because of him."

Daniel swore under his breath.

"He knew it was dangerous for me to get pregnant again, but by then that was my only purpose in life, as far as he was concerned. Barefoot and pregnant in the kitchen." She dashed angry tears from her eyes. "I had completed all my training, finished my student teaching, and all the while he was trying to get me pregnant. I expected to stop work when I had babies, I did, but I never thought I'd have three children in less than three years. Then when I did get pregnant again so soon, the doctor said I needed bed rest. Samuel knew, but he didn't care, just cared about me having food on the table and warming his bed. And I lost her. My little girl."

The tears poured out, and Daniel gathered her in his arms, pressed her forehead to his chest and simply held her.

She dragged in air between the words. "I told you I couldn't have any more children. When they went to do the D and C, too much of my womb was damaged and they took it out." Another sob shook her. "I know it seems so silly to be upset about it in light of the fact he used to hit me, but..."

He stopped dead in his tracks. He tried to put as much tenderness as possible into the kiss he pressed to her temple.

"It's the farthest thing from silly. I bet you've got people who tell you that you should count your blessings, right? That you've got three fine boys, and what more could you want." He laughed, knowing that it sounded hollow. He buried his fingers in her hair and pulled her gaze up to meet his own. "It doesn't take away the hurt. You love them nonetheless, but the ones that you can't have, because the decision wasn't yours—

"It hurts like blue blazes and there's nothing anyone can say that's ever going to make it feel better. A piece of your future is dead, and yet people walk on all around you and expect you to keep going when there's nothing but a fucking hole in front of you—as if you're the only one who sees it."

The dark centers of her eyes glistened with her unshed tears. "Oh, Daniel."

He held her. Gently. His lips touching her forehead, and her cheek, and her lashes. Trying to pass over an inkling of compassion that she could appreciate and comprehend in the midst of her hurts.

Beth tangled her fingers in his hair and kissed him. She held their mouths together until the kiss faded away, and they hung, lip to lip, air mingling as they attempted to balance their breathing.

He pulled her into his lap, lifting her to straddle his legs. His hand caressed her back, massaging the muscles as he clutched her close, their torsos tight as they continued to touch and comfort each other.

Beth curved a hand down the side of his face and tentatively brushed a tear that clung to the edge of his eye. "I'm so sorry."

"I'm sorry too. I know part of your pain." He took a deep breath and stared into her eyes. "As far as your husband is concerned? There's a special place in hell reserved for men like him. If he hadn't died, things might have gotten worse and you could be the one dead now. Or one of your sons..."

His throat closed off at the thought of any of the towheaded boys tangled in their beds down the hall being hurt.

Beth held his face, and he could have drowned in her tear-filled eyes. Barely above a whisper, she spoke as she caressed his bristle-roughed cheek. "I know we have so much more to discuss, but I need you. Need you to chase away the pain, just for a little while."

They moved together, willing accomplices. Lips and tongues tangling, taking turns to slip off their remaining clothing as they shrugged shoulders and wiggled limbs. When she stripped bare from the waist up, Daniel took possession of one firm nipple, cupping her breast and lifting it to his lips to suck.

"So good." Beth let her head drop back.

"I want you tonight. All of you."

He made love to her that night. Lifted her and placed her with such care on the bed. Tugged off her panties slowly, careful of her aching limbs. Somehow between kissing every inch of her body and arranging her naked form on the bed, he shucked his jeans. Beth looked up from where she lay, the moonlight pouring in the window to illuminate every muscular inch of his body. His cock rose from the tight curls at his groin, and he slipped over her, the heat of his torso rolling ahead like a steamroller and pinning her in place.

"Tonight, you're mine. No games, no playing. Just open yourself up and give yourself to me, Beth. Let go and let me catch you."

Her throat was tight as he suspended himself over her, thigh to thigh, nose to nose. His eyes, oh damn—his eyes were beautiful. Full of tenderness and need, and she wrapped her arms around his torso and pulled him down, sighing as his bare skin touched hers, as if for the first time.

They touched and moved together, in perfect harmony. He kissed her mouth, her breasts, the indent of her belly. He licked her clit, and she opened wide, letting him touch her everywhere, as hard as he liked, as soft as he wanted. Her first orgasm surprised them both as she rocked with the initial touch of his hand to her pussy. He moved over her while her sheath still convulsed and with one firm motion joined them. He locked their hips together, pulling her head to his, lips and tongues tasting and embroiled with white-hot need. Then he started, slow, minute pulses of his hips that dragged his cock back an inch before reburying him deep. Deeper yet as she pulled up her knees and spread herself wide.

"God, Beth, yes." His strokes hesitated for a moment, uneven and broken in rhythm.

"Do it. Come on...oh there, so good. You feel so good inside me. All I need, I..."

She wanted to confess with words what their bodies were

saying but she refrained, instead staring into his eyes and saying it the best she could. It was love. It was physical connection that went soul deep and tears welled up as he stared. Another thrust, another. The rubbing intensified, every nerve on fire. He grasped her nipple and sucked hard, and the spear of pain shot into pleasure that radiated over her skin, throbbing in her sheath. She grabbed his head and drew their mouths together again, needing the connection, needing to taste him. She bit his lower lip and licked the pain away as he erased the pain lingering in her heart. No, not erased, but eased. They were together, they belonged together.

The bed creaked in an easy rhythm and he groaned over her. "So close. You need to come. I want to feel you around me. Squeezing me. Surrounding me." He adjusted the angle of her body, lifting her hips higher, tilting his pelvis up to thrust harder, more forcibly. The cool air moved over her clit when his body pulled away. Then he touched her, his fingers rubbing firmly and the pulse of sensation broke free.

"*Yes...*" She clutched his neck tight and gave herself up to pleasure. Let it roll like the fall wind over the prairies. A second later he joined her, his harsh breathing giving way to a contented sigh as he jerked inside her, the heat of his release bathing her.

"Yes, oh damn." He dropped his head on her shoulder, covering her with his body, and she didn't even try to stop the tears.

"That was perfect," she whispered.

He rolled them carefully, drawing her on top so they stayed intimately connected. His tender caress and consideration made her heart ache.

He rubbed her back, dragged his hands through her hair again and again, until their breathing calmed and only the rapid beat of his heart gave away the fact they'd been running a marathon in bed. He chuckled softly, as if he was aware of keeping the noise down.

"Perfect, eh?"

"Hmm, I think." The languid sensation stealing through her limbs made it tough to fight the sleep now creeping up.

"Even though it was missionary vanilla sex?"

Something twigged in her brain, and suddenly it was funny as anything. She was an emotional yo-yo. A giggle escaped, then the giggle escalated to a snicker. She took a deep breath, still shaky from the bombshells of the evening. Daniel rolled them to their sides, keeping their bodies close and their spirits together as they snuggled under the covers.

Chapter Sixteen

"Mom. Mooooom."

The rattling at the doorknob jolted her awake, and she slipped out a hand in search of Daniel. She could have sworn only seconds before he'd been wrapped around her, kissing her neck and whispering loving things in her ear.

The bed beside her was still warm.

"Mom—mie."

Beth sat up, clutching the sheet to her chest as she looked around the room in confusion. The very empty room. She glanced at the window then laughed. No, he hadn't dove out that way.

"Just a minute. Mommy's getting up."

She pulled on her sleep shirt before unlocking the door. Nathan and Robbie swarmed in and dragged her back to the bed for snuggles. Lance strolled in slower, almost suspiciously, and she fought to keep from blushing. That wasn't in the cards yet, to try to explain to her eight-year-old why there was a man in his mom's bed.

And yet...why not? Would the boys not understand that Daniel was someone who made her very happy? Who maybe, possibly, could make them happy too?

She pondered the question the whole time the kids rattled on about what they'd done with him the day before. While they helped make breakfast and while she cleaned up the mess afterward. It wasn't until she finished cleaning she spotted the note he'd left for her propped up beside the phone.

I'm on early chores in the barn. I'll stop by to see you later. Take you out for a coffee?

Her mom's question came back: If Daniel was someone she was truly going to trust, how was she going to let him know? Show him, and herself, she thought he was worthy of being trusted. Last night she'd shared things with him she'd never told another person. Did he understand how difficult that had been? What it meant to have felt she could tell him— everything? She'd already done something huge by leaving him alone with her boys. There wasn't a much more tangible way of saying she trusted him than that.

But she hadn't verbally said it, and she hadn't said what was in her heart. And after dictating what she expected of this relationship all those months ago, if she was going to change the rules, she needed to tell him.

She made a quick phone call then called to the boys to get their things together.

"Where we going?" Lance checked the clock and frowned. "It's too early for swimming."

"Not too early for a visit. It's Saturday, and Mr. Coleman said he needed you to show him where the kittens are you found yesterday."

Squeals of delight rose and Beth smiled. Yes, and Marion Coleman needed to show them how to bake and eat too many cookies. And the rest of the Coleman boys needed to teach them how brothers could love and support each other even if they didn't always see eye to eye on everything. How to be a family, with strong men who weren't afraid to love their women wholeheartedly.

She blinked back the tears and hustled everyone out the door, desperately trying to figure exactly what she was going to say to Daniel when she finally saw him.

It was poetic she found him in the barn, the same place she'd searched him out three months earlier. He wandered from stall to stall, pouring grain from a bag. One of the horses sniffed his hair and made little nickering sounds. Daniel laughed, reaching up to rub its nose, the easy way he moved speaking of his familiarity with the animals and his patience. Her physical pull toward him was incredible, even in dirty jeans with his hair all mussed. She'd never seen him look more attractive, except maybe the previous night when he'd cradled Nathan so carefully.

She took a deep breath. "Hey."

He swung around and his face lit up.

"Good morning, darling." He strode forward and took her in his arms, planting a juicy kiss on her lips before he paused and released her, glancing around in embarrassment. "Shit, sorry. I didn't even think to check if the boys were with you."

"They're at your parents' house."

"With my folks?" He frowned in confusion.

She twisted her fingers together, shy and nervous again. "You got a minute? We need to talk." Damn, how often had she said that? Or him to her?

He smiled. "I feel as if we're caught in one of those time warps. You want to walk or sit here in the barn with me?"

They laughed together, and suddenly she wasn't anxious anymore. She tucked herself back against his body, resting her head on his chest. "I missed waking up in your arms this morning."

He kissed her forehead. "I didn't want to push it with the boys, but damn you were hard to leave."

Beth looked into his eyes, marveling at the way he waited patiently for her to make the next move. To speak. She really did feel safe with him. "Remember when I said that I wasn't looking for a long-term relationship and you said we had to be friends as well as lovers?"

"Yeah."

"Do you feel as if we're friends?"

Daniel held her for a minute, staring off into space over her head. Her mind darted with the possibilities of his response. Was she pushing too fast? Then he lifted her chin so their eyes met. She could see the caring on his face.

"I think in some ways we are, and others, we're still learning." He shook his head. "I can't believe that I never knew about your husband. I should have been so much more careful with you, so much gentler."

He had been. "Oh, Daniel, everything you did was right, even if it was by accident. All our early visits were out in public, and you pushed my comfort levels the right way. You were yourself. I got to see how you dealt with the people around you, see what they thought of you. There was no pretending with you, ever. I don't think I could have been comfortable so quickly with anyone else."

"Do you think we're friends?" he asked.

She kissed him. "With benefits." He stiffened, and she hurried on before all her hard-won courage failed. "But it's not enough. Not anymore." She stepped back so she could look him straight in the eye. "I think I'm falling in love with you."

"Oh, thank God."

His completely unexpected reaction made the last bubble of fear burst and joy well up in its place. She laughed out loud. "Daniel Coleman, you are impossible. What's that supposed to mean?"

He picked her up and spun her around in a circle, clasping her close. "Just that it's a good thing to know you're falling, because when you land, I'll be there waiting for you. I fell awhile ago, and I've been hoping you'd catch up."

"Are you saying—?"

"I love you. I think the world of you and how you've faced your fears and made a new life for yourself and the boys. The way you smile and laugh, the way you pour yourself into your kids at home and at the school." He set her back on her feet and wrapped his arms around her torso, pressing their bodies together. "I love the way you feel under me, and yet sex is a small part of it. I love the whole package, Miss Beth."

She hugged him tightly as he spoke. He loved her. She could see it in his eyes and hear it in his voice, and every bit of it rang true.

"So...what now?" she asked. He led her to a bale, and once again the coincidence of the situation hit her hard. They settled next to each other, hands linked.

"If it were just you and me involved here, I'd be willing to do whatever you feel needs to be done. I'd go down on one knee and propose if that's what you wanted. I'd move in with you, and we could be partners for the rest of our lives without the need for any piece of paper or fancy words being spoken. But what about the boys?"

She lifted their joined hands to her lips and kissed his knuckles. It was so like Daniel to try to think the whole thing through. If she could be any surer, that would have been the final nudge she needed, that he was concerned about her sons.

He was the one they all needed in their lives, for better or worse.

Daniel could barely breathe, the raw emotion running through his body drawing his throat tight. He was looking at the possibility of forever hovering in front of him, and damn if he could figure out the right move to make.

"The way I see it, those kids have been through an awful lot over the past year, and they must be pretty confused. You were hurt pretty bad in the accident, and suddenly their daddy was gone. Yeah, the man wasn't a good father, but he was still all they knew. You moved them to a new home and new schools, new friends. All that for the best of reasons, but it has got to make their heads spin. They might not take kindly to me coming in as someone other than a temporary babysitter."

Beth shook her head. "I want what is best for my boys, but that doesn't mean letting them dictate what I do with my life. It's not going to be all sweetness and roses trying to make them understand who you will be in their lives, but just because they balk a few times doesn't mean it's not the best thing for them."

"But should we push them too fast? Do we have to push them?"

"What are you suggesting? That we carry on like we have?"

"Hell no. I'm done with the hiding, and I thought you'd made it pretty clear the other day at the bar we were together. The boys can get used to the idea of me being around, slowly. It's only a couple of weeks until Christmas, and while I want to be in your life and theirs, I don't see any reason to rush it now."

"So...we date?"

"Yup. You stay in the house with the boys for a while longer. Then I have another plan I've been working on, but I need your help with the numbers to make sure it's possible. I've been chatting with Blake and Travis about buying out their portions of the furniture shop. Neither of them is interested in continuing, they'd much rather work the land and deal with that side of the ranch. I'm ready for a change and willing to sell them my share. I thought about finding a place right in town, a house. I think I've got enough money saved up, although I'd want to get my daddy's blessing before heading into a new venture."

She looked shocked. "You don't want to ranch anymore?"

"Nope. Not if I can afford to change tracks."

She laughed. "Daniel, we need to go somewhere, just the two of us and actually sit and talk for a couple days straight. How come I didn't know you wanted to get out of ranching?"

He tweaked her nose. "Because we were too busy trying every non-vanilla experience we could think of."

"True."

They sat in silence for a minute.

"My mom offered to watch the kids."

"Jaxi offered to watch..."

They spoke simultaneously then broke off.

Daniel grinned. "Heck, I bet half of Rocky would offer to watch the kids to let us have a getaway."

"You honestly want to move into town?"

"Hell, yeah. Beth, I loved growing up on the ranch, and I love my family, but I feel as if I need to take the next step. What better time than now? We could find a house we both like close to the school for the kids. Easy for you to get to work." *Crap,* there was another example of how little he knew. "Hell, I don't even know if you still want to work if you don't have to."

They both took a deep breath and leaned together closer, her arms draped around his neck.

Beth shook her head. "This is one the strangest situations I've ever heard of. We love each other, but we're going to take it slow for a while longer, until we can actually say that we're friends?"

"Sounds about right to me." He lifted her chin. "How long my folks thinking they got the boys for today?"

"Before I left, your dad had agreed to take over your duties at the pool today and your mom was asking what their favourite supper was. Does that sound like the whole day to you?"

Oh yeah. "How about we go back to the house, grab whatever you need and head out for a while? Spend some time doing some serious talking and planning and dreaming."

"You don't want to stay home?" There was a hint of mischief in her eyes.

"Only if you promise not to jump me."

"What?" Beth laughed as he pulled her to her feet.

Daniel held her hands in his, rubbing his fingers over her knuckles. "Us getting alone has usually meant sex up to now. We need more. If we can keep from getting distracted, then the house would be fine. We'll light the fire and cuddle on the couch and talk each other's ears off. And hopefully by the time we head over to join my folks for supper, we'll have an idea of how we're going to explain our plan to the boys."

Beth squeezed his hand. "I'm looking forward to becoming your friend."

The hopeful expression in her eyes made the future seem damn bright.

Chapter Seventeen

"How much longer you think the boys are going to last?"

Beth turned and smiled at Daniel's whispered question. "Robbie is a goner already, and Nathan probably won't be too far behind. But you know Lance is going to try to stay awake until the last possible second."

The noise from the Wii filled the room as Blake and Lance fought another pitched battle. On the couch next to them, Nathan leaned against Jaxi's side, her arm holding him vertical more than any power of his own.

New Year's Eve, and the party was so much milder than any he'd attended in a long, long time. It was also the most exciting ever because Beth and the boys were there with his family.

Jaxi adjusted Nathan then cheered Lance on. "Get him. Knock him out of there, Lance. That's it. Sweet..."

"Hey, that's enough. Stop pulling for the enemy. I'm your husband, you're supposed to want me to win," Blake complained.

Jaxi stuck out her tongue, and Lance snorted, then destroyed another of Blake's strongholds.

Daniel held his hand to Beth, and she took it. Jaxi wiggled her fingers in farewell as they snuck out of the basement, up the stairs to the main living room.

"It's a quiet New Year's. I hope this isn't disappointing to you." Beth slipped her hand around his back and tugged him to stop before they lost their privacy.

"Disappointing? No way." He fit his hand around her nape and held her close, staring into her eyes. "Try perfect. I've been worried the past couple weeks might have been overwhelming for the boys and you, since the entire clan has been around all the time. What with spare Colemans popping in and out at random moments without any warning, I wondered when you were going to turn and run for the hills."

Beth cupped his face in her hand, her thumb gently stroking back and forth over his cheek. The smile she gave him was real and content and made his soul satisfied. "How could you even think that for a moment? The Christmas holidays have been filled with one wonderful experience after the other for the boys and me. Your family is incredible."

They kissed, lips gentle and soft against each other. Tongues dipping and brushing, nothing panicked or rushed. Just a comfortable and celebratory motion that said more about belonging to each other than ownership.

Daniel savoured it even as he made plans for some ownership kind of sex later that night. He liked having both sides in their relationship, and Beth was still enjoying the lessons.

Damn, his life was good.

He pulled away and gave her a wink. "What do you think about having that conversation with my folks now?"

"Tonight? But it's New Year's Eve...?"

"As good a time as any for making plans for the future. Ain't this when you're supposed to do up resolutions?" He wasn't sure what he was going to see in her eyes, but the sheer joy reflecting out took him by surprise. "I like that expression,

Miss Beth. You gonna tell me what's going on in that pretty head of yours to make you look all shiny like that?"

She squeezed his neck so hard he thought he heard a crack.

"You are the best man I've ever met. It's as if you..."

Beth pulled away and composed herself for a moment.

He waited. With what was written on her face, this wasn't anything he wanted to miss out on having her share.

"I can't even explain it. Telling you I love you seems inadequate. I love your family and how they've welcomed us in. Things like your parents having my folks over at Christmas, making sure everyone was friendly and accepting—you can't understand what a gift that was after how my husband treated them for years."

"Bastard."

She pressed her fingers to his lips. "And I'm not bringing him up except to point out how much better this is. Richer. Warmer. Safer. So if you think it's time for the next stage of the game, I trust you."

The light in her face didn't only shine out and turn her ten kinds of beautiful, it warmed him through and through.

They slipped into the living room, hand in hand.

His ma lifted her head, and he caught another glimpse of family that made him even happier. Robbie was curled up in her lap, body draped against her, hair wild as he slumbered.

"I told you he'd be asleep already." Beth squeezed Daniel's fingers and made as if to release him. He held on tight and tugged her across to the couch between his parents' recliners.

"You're not stealing him away yet, are you?" Marion Coleman rocked slowly, adjusting her grasp on the boy, her smile growing wider if anything.

"You're not going to get him out of her arms without a crowbar, I'm thinking." Mike's chair squeaked slightly as he slid forward and headed to the liquor bottles on the side table. "Either of you want a drink? It's a quiet party, I know, but we're able to have a celebration of our own right here. Not as wild as what the rest of your brothers are up to, I bet."

"I'm having a wonderful time, Dad. No need for the noise and craziness to make me happy."

Beth's bright laugh was quiet enough to not wake Robbie. "As if it was anything that could be considered quiet in here earlier. I'm sorry, Marion, the boys were so excited at dinner, I really didn't..."

"Hush." Marion waved her fingers in dismissal. "Trust me, they were nothing on our six back in the day. And frankly, I think it was mainly Blake and Daniel causing all the ruckus tonight, and not your angels."

Daniel bit his lip as he accepted a glass from his father. Yeah, the noise of laughing and happiness wasn't something he'd complain about. That wasn't the part he wanted to change, and that's what he had to make clear.

"You folks okay if I bring up a question I've got? Regarding the ranch?"

Mike and Marion exchanged glances.

His dad sat back down and looked over at the couch, examining Beth and Daniel closely. "Sounds serious."

Daniel took a deep breath. "Serious but nothing too worrisome, I hope. I've wanted to run something past you for a while, and I think I've got the numbers figured out. You know how you mentioned it might get tight when the twins finished school? Trying to support everyone on the profits from the ranch?"

His dad sipped his drink. He nodded—didn't say anything

though, and for a moment Daniel hesitated.

Just because his dreams lay in a different direction didn't mean the ranch wasn't a fabulous place to make a living. This change wasn't supposed to be a poor reflection on his father or his abilities.

"You've done good, Dad. Real good over the years, in the decisions you've made. Things like setting up the workshop and diversifying our livestock. You've never stood still and that's why we've done so well. But with the changes in the market, you're right. Finances will get tight, and I doubt there's any way the ranch can support seven families, if at some point we all settle down. It's not like in Grampa's day—we can't split the land any more without losing the advantage of having a big parcel. So I've been wondering—what would you think of me moving into something else?"

"You want to leave the ranch?" Marion rocked her chair steadily, sadness on her face.

"Not to move far away. If I was to run the workshop full time, I could actually increase the orders we take in. There's the possibility we could end up making more money than we are now, but I've got to be full time in the shop. Juggling two major endeavors would just get us in trouble."

Mike's slow smile eased Daniel's fears. The twinkle of amusement that flashed in his father's eyes a moment later piqued his curiosity.

"You know, it's funny to watch you and your brothers tiptoe around me. I never thought I was the intimidating kind of father, but heck if you all don't still take it real careful anyway."

Daniel looked him in eye. The confession was easy to make. "It's not that we're afraid of you, it's that we respect you."

The pleasure on Mike's face was easy to read. He coughed lightly for a moment, taking a sip of his drink before continuing.

"You've obviously given this a lot of consideration."

"I have." The words spilled out now that Daniel had started. "And while I've loved working with you over the years, I just don't enjoy ranching like you do, sir. Not like Blake and Travis especially. Or maybe I should put it the other way. I enjoy the woodworking so much more, and since I think there's a viable living there, I want to propose a buyout."

"Well, I can't say as this is a real surprise to me. Before we make any firm decisions, I need to see some numbers. But, son, it's your life and you've got to be doing what's going to make you happy. If it works financially to all our advantage, who am I to say no? You still think on keeping the shop here? Or moving her to a new location—?"

"Enough." Marion broke in. "You can talk through all that later. I want to know the important stuff first. Like, where do you plan on living, and it had better not be too far away."

"Ma." Daniel grinned at her. "I'm not thinking about going anywhere except maybe into town."

She wrinkled her nose then shrugged. "You're the one who's got to live there, so I won't mention how much you'll miss hearing the frogs in the spring. Always your favourite thing."

He snorted. "I'm never going to be more than five years old to you, am I?"

Marion shook her head, her gaze darting over Beth. The questions were there in her eyes, but she held her tongue, and Daniel was grateful. Yeah, he had ideas that direction as well, but it wasn't the place or the time. Yet.

The New Year was going to bring all kinds of wonderful things to him—to *them*—and he could hardly wait.

Chapter Eighteen

The look of disgust on his brother's face made Gabe's lips twitch as he fought to hide his amusement.

"It's just mean." Rafe growled out the words before twisting away and heading for the door.

Gabe felt for him, but there was not much he could do. "Don't pout. You heard Dad as clear as I did—you're working with him first thing in the morning. Going to a party tonight isn't going to fly. Unless you think you're good to get up at four a.m. and be alert enough to—"

Rafe kicked the garbage pail by the edge of the kitchen sink, the metal clanking as it struck the counter. The discord of the echo bounced off the walls of Gabe's apartment like an out-of-tune cymbal. "I know why I can't go out. Just, there's all week to do the repairs in the barns. I don't see any reason we've got to put in such an early day tomorrow."

There was no reason Gabe could give him. No reason other than their dad had made the decision to work like a maniac, which meant they had to as well. "It sucks, but it's life. Find something else to do tonight. Call someone. Text them, or organize a game online, or something."

Rafe gave him another dirty look. "It's New Year's Eve. I *had* plans, remember? They're all cancelled since I'm not allowed to grab a truck to get into town, and you're being a shit and refusing to take me along with you."

His kid brother might be feeling the weight of the world right now, but it wasn't going to change Gabe's mind. "Sorry, I highly doubt a seventeen-year-old would be welcome where I'm going. And besides, you're operating machinery in the morning. I'm not keeping you up until all hours and then putting you behind the wheel."

All the air went out of Raphael as he leaned unhappily against the door. "You sure you don't want to stay home and play cards with me for a couple hours? It's New Year's Eve and I'm headed to bed like a baby. Having you stick around would make it a whole lot better."

"I've got plans."

Rafe wouldn't look him in the eye, and Gabe felt like the shit his brother had called him. It had to be miserable, but the reality was their dad still had the right to call the shots in the kid's life.

Heck, in his life too, at least as it related to the ranch.

He'd been researching the best he could during downtimes from working. There was much to learn, and Gabe wasn't about to bring up the idea of changes until he could make the benefits clear to their father.

So for now, they ran things the old-fashioned way. Which meant their father Ben was in charge, with no discussion, no arguments. Gabe, and Rafe when he was out of school, were the obedient labour.

Gabe sighed. "It's a hell of a thing, but at least you know dad will be slaving just as hard as us all week. He's just got...unusual timing."

Rafe groaned and slouched harder.

Inspiration struck. "Hey, you want to crash out here tonight?"

Rafe looked up from under his bangs. "In your apartment?"

"Sure. I'll be home late, but you can use the bedroom, and I'll hit the couch when I get in. I don't mind."

Maybe a little space to himself would make up for some of his brother's disappointment.

"Well, it's not the party, but since I didn't actually have a date..." Rafe straightened, his normal enthusiasm returning in a rush. "Can I have a few beers?"

Gabe resisted the urge to roll his eyes. "One, since part of the reason for you to stay home is so you're not hungover in the morning. Go—grab your stuff, and I'll call Mom and let her know what's happening. I'm sure she'll be fine with it. She can smooth it over with Dad. Just, for God's sake, set the damn alarm and don't bloody well sleep in."

Rafe raced out the door and across the distance to the main house, without pulling on his abandoned winter coat, and Gabe shook his head. Oh, to be young and full of energy, bouncing back that quickly from disappointment.

A couple hours later Gabe was wishing he'd stayed at home with Rafe.

He stepped over another couple on the floor groping each other madly and wondered where the hell all the bodies had come from. Debauchery was alive and well at the turn of the year.

"Happy Fuckin' New Year."

The call echoed back from a dozen throats too inebriated to enunciate properly. Gabe shook his head and wondered why he'd even bothered coming.

Because a twenty-nine-year-old sitting alone at home with

his kid brother on New Year's Eve is beyond pathetic?

There were small pockets of sanity scattered throughout the room. Even though they both had a woman on their laps, the Six Pack twins were sober enough to be holding a verbal contest with a few other guys, including two of the Moonshine Colemans. Hell, everywhere he looked there were Colemans sprinkled in amidst the rest of the partiers. The notable absences were the Whiskey Creek girls, Blake, Daniel, and his own brother, Rafe.

Gabe eyed the room, feeling far wearier than he should. Maybe he would head home early.

A hand slapped on his shoulder, and he twirled to face Matt. Great, just what he needed. *Not.*

"You've become a bit of recluse, cousin." Matt gave him a tired smile before turning his gaze back into the room behind them.

Awkwardness had settled between him and Matt ever since he'd seen Helen in Red Deer and kept it to himself. Maybe he'd been wrong in his suspicions, but the whole thing never sat right after.

"I was thinking about packing it in. Not in a partying mood tonight since the chores are gonna be there in the morning no matter what time I hit the sack."

Matt grimaced. "I hear you. I'm on first shift too, in spite of Blake being snuggled up early with Jaxi."

"Yeah, well, you're assuming they're going to sleep, and that's probably bullshit."

His cousin nodded. "Hey, before you go, help me find Helen, will you? She'd been putting the drinks back pretty hard before we even came out, and now she's gone missing. I haven't seen her for nearly an hour."

"She didn't go outside, did she?"

"Nahhh, her coat and boots are still here, but I've looked around the house once already. I wonder if I'm walking in a circle and missing her."

Gabe headed the direction Matt aimed him, unwilling to suggest that if Helen was shitfaced, her coat and boots being left behind were no indication of anything good. She'd be far more likely to go wandering outside without them while drunk.

Music shredded his eardrums. The driving pulse echoed off the walls and competed with raised voices. Lighting was low throughout the old house, the main residence for the oldest two cousins on the Moonshine side of the Coleman clan. They lived with a couple friends, and while he'd been offered a place with them, Gabe had easily turned down the invitation. His tiny apartment wasn't fabulous, but it was better than living in this kind of raucous chaos on a regular basis.

He paused outside a closed bedroom door, suddenly awkward. The things he did for family...

Gabe knocked, got no answer, then pushed the door open to make sure Helen wasn't passed out on the floor or something. The first room was empty, and he breathed a sigh of relief. All his Zen-like calm vanished a moment later when he swung open the master bedroom door and froze.

He'd found her.

There was a second music system playing in the room, the drums in the current song pulsing out a tempo echoed in the sexual display before him.

If it had been anyone other than Helen, he might have thought the scene was hot—maybe even stepped closer to get a better view. He had no issues with a woman taking control of her sexuality. No matter now dirty, rough or how many partners she wanted, it was her own damn business.

But this was *Helen.*

She stood on the far side of the room, hair hanging down. Her naked body undulated to the music as she displayed herself like some go-go dancer in a racy nightclub to the men seated in front of her. One of them pulled her forward, pushing her to her knees as he stood. Helen fumbled at his zipper, reaching in and exposing his cock. She pumped him hard a couple times before plunging her mouth over his dick and taking him deep.

Gabe had seen enough. His only remaining brain cells still working focused entirely on one thing.

Matt. What the hell was Matt going to do?

There was no question of hiding this—the concern was keeping murder from happening. Because Gabe felt ready to strangle someone, and she wasn't even his woman.

Four steps brought him across the distance as he reacted without thinking, fist landing hard to the jaw of the man standing before Helen. The guy's head snapped back and he spun off to lie stunned on the floor with his dick still hanging from his jeans.

"What the fuck you doing?" One of the strangers leaned over his fallen friend briefly before turning to face Gabe.

"Gabe?" Helen pushed herself upright, swaying drunkenly. "Hmm, you gonna have some fun tonight too?"

This wasn't the sweet woman he'd cared for a few months ago with his cousin—this was some out-of-control creature. But for Matt's sake, he had to get her dressed. Get her out here.

Gabe grabbed her under the arms and bodily lifted her, moving away from the impromptu stage. "I don't give a damn who you guys are or who invited you. Get the hell out of here."

"Fuck off."

The remaining guys got up swinging. Trying to keep Helen behind him hindered Gabe from escaping completely. Not that he cared right then if she got tangled in the fight—don't hang with the crows if you don't want to get shot—but...

Matt.

What a bloody mess.

Gabe ducked another punch and got in a couple solid blows of his own before everything went to shit and the room filled with people.

Including Matt.

It was like watching death overtake a person, the way the colour stripped from Matt's face. There wasn't much to see anymore—Gabe had no idea what Matt thought had gone down, and he wasn't about to say anything until there were fewer people around to hear.

Matt scrambled past the few bodies between them and caught Helen against him. Someone grabbed a blanket to cover her, as she alternated between weeping and cussing.

"Okay, back to the party. There's nothing to see, everything's fine." Steve and Trevor, the oldest Moonshine Colemans, cleared the room of the newcomers quick enough, but there was still hell to be paid if the expression on Matt's face was anything to go on.

Helen wouldn't stop crying, and Gabe wanted nothing better to slap some sense into her. There was no reason for her to make that kind of commotion.

Gabe tilted his head toward the three men and whispered quickly to Steve, "Get them out now."

"Wait." Matt's voice was soft and icy cold. "I want to know what the fuck was going on."

Joel had slipped into the room and stood beside Matt, a

frown creasing his forehead even as his fists tightened. Gabe shook his head and motioned for him to stay put.

One of the strangers answered. "Just a little fun, is all. She said she wanted to—"

"Helen?"

The weeping had finally stopped, and Matt stared at her, shock and hurt in his face. She wiped her eyes and swallowed, then shoved him from her sharply. She rocked on her feet unsteadily, the blanket falling from her shoulders to reveal her nakedness to the entire room. "My idea. Wanted some fun—"

"Fun?" The word tore from Matt's lips like a knife slash. "You're wasted. Where are your clothes? I'll take you home."

"Fuck you. I'm not going anywhere. Want to stay. Want to—" She teetered and Gabe grabbed her, snatching the blanket from the floor and forcing it around her shoulders.

"Matt, what's going on?" Joel wasn't the only one confused.

"My girlfriend is drunk."

"Not drunk. Want to stay. Get some excitement in my life. Because you? Matt Coleman? You're boring. No fun."

A sharp hiss escaped Matt.

Trevor pushed the strangers from the room. Steve kept a close eye on them, motioning with his head from the doorway. "We've got them taken care of. Take your time—I'll see that this stays as quiet as possible. Get everyone partying again."

With one last sympathetic glance Matt's direction, Steve closed the door.

"Matt..." Gabe wasn't sure what to do. What to say.

Matt stared at Helen, something dark in his expression. "You fooling around on me, Helen?"

She stared back. No denial.

Oh God.

Joel wrapped an arm around Matt and pulled him away. "Leave it for now. She's pissed to the gills, and you're angry. Let me take her home and you can talk it out when she's sober—"

"Screw you, Jesse Coleman. Or Joel, or whoever the hell you are. This is none of your damn business. We don't need to leave anything for any time." Helen struggled upright and stared at Matt, clinging to the blanket around her shoulders. She lifted her chin and glared him down, eyes glazed from too much drink. "I'm leaving town. I got a new job that starts in a week. I'm never coming back to this godforsaken hellhole that you've tried to convince me is the be-all and end-all of the universe. It's not. It was a shitty place to grow up and a shitty place to live, and I'm not going to stay any longer. So you can take your Six Pack and your *I love you*s, and you can stick them up your ass. Because I'm getting out of here before I die of boredom."

Gabe had never hit a woman in his life. Never wanted to, but in that moment, seeing the pain that rippled through Matt, he was sorely tempted.

Matt turned on his heel and left.

There was quiet for a moment before Joel stepped close enough to force Helen's chin up so she had to look him in eye.

"You're a selfish, spoiled bitch. I suggest you sober up real fast and get out of town. Far out of town, because there's no way you're going to ever be able to make this better." Joel glanced over at Gabe. "Sorry for leaving you with the garbage to clean up. I'm going after Matt."

Silence fell over the room as the door clicked shut behind him. Gabe moved as far away as possible as Helen quietly looked for her clothes.

If she said so much as one word wrong, he was liable to

wring her neck.

He snuck her out the back door and drove her home, all without talking. He was caught up in wondering if he could have stopped the disaster from happening by speaking to Matt sooner, but he'd been blinded by his own plans. Guilt at his mistake made the situation worse, if anything could make this worse.

He stopped outside her apartment, the new one she'd recently moved into with her sister overtop the shop they were supposed to open come the spring. There was another thing she'd lied about. Gabe stared forward, willing her to leave before rage made him toss her on her ass.

She stepped out, the fresh snow and her drunken footing making her weave to the apartment door. He forced himself to wait until she'd disappeared from sight, because if he'd left before he knew she was safely inside and she froze to death, he'd find it hard to feel remorse.

A part inside him had gone colder than the temperature outside. It was stupid the way his brain leapt from point to point, connecting lines that maybe shouldn't be there, but still insistently depressing. All his wonderful plans for the ranch, all his striving to find a better future for his family—doubts racked him. His cousin Matt had done everything he could to make Helen happy, and this was the result?

On the dashboard clock, the digital display had clicked over to midnight sometime in the past few minutes, and it was as if a knife turned in his heart.

Happy fucking New Year.

Chapter Nineteen

"Go fish."

Beth shook her head and pulled over another pile of marking, thankful that for once it wasn't her having to play the game for the twenty-millionth time.

Only when the delighted squealing died away for long enough, she got suspicious. She rose from her desk and snuck her head around the corner to find out what her guys were up to.

Her guys. The words made her smile.

They were all seated around the table, crayons scattered everywhere. Nathan had his tongue hanging out a little, all his focus and concentration on whatever it was in front of him.

Robbie spotted her and covered his paper with his arms. "Moo—oom. No peeking."

Daniel winked as she held up her hands and retreated around the corner. "Sorry, didn't mean to pry. I'll get back to work."

"Kitchen is off limits for a while, Beth. I've got things under control." Daniel stepped around the corner. "How much marking you got left?"

"An hour or so." Beth looked him up and down in admiration. He was wearing new jeans, the dark colour crisp and sharp. His cotton overshirt was neatly tucked in at the waist, and she wanted to tug it free. Wanted to slip her fingers under the soft fabric of his T-shirt and dip under the waistband to caress the firm ridge of muscle that separated his groin from his thigh.

She loved that muscle on him.

"When you're done, why don't you sneak upstairs and have a bath. We'll give you a heads-up for supper." Daniel grinned as her smile got wider.

A bath? "Well, aren't you just spoiling me to pieces?"

He glanced over his shoulder before stepping all the way to her side and cupping her face for a quick kiss. The warmth of his body crossed the short distance between them, and she had to refrain from rubbing against him like a lovesick cat.

He pulled back then brushed her lower lip with his thumb. "I think if you look beside your bed there might be something you could use during your spa getaway."

The quietly spoken words made her more curious than ever. "Now I'm going to rush my marking and someone out there is going to be eternally grateful that they didn't get the D minus they deserve."

Daniel backed away one step at a time, his gaze never leaving hers, his teasing grin that warmed her inside promising more mischief later.

The sounds from the kitchen, little-boy whispers loud enough to hear clearly from a room away, kept the grin on her own face firmly in place. Luckily the schoolwork she had to complete wasn't difficult, because her concentration was shot to hell.

When she finally tucked her paperwork away and snuck upstairs, the kitchen noises had changed to include banging pots and giggles. Daniel's occasional deep rumble of laughter reassured her, and she headed into her room to change and discover her surprise.

There was a red gift bag waiting on the dresser. She held off her curiosity long enough to strip and put on her robe, walk across the landing to the bath and lock herself in. With the water running, she dug into the bag and one-at-a-time pulled out treasures obviously wrapped by her sons. Bath beads, an oversized loofah brush with the head of a surprised giraffe—had to be from Nathan. A bottle of bright blue nail polish. Beth laughed with delight.

A plethora of Valentine's love poured out for her. She tossed a bead into the filling tub and eased herself into the water, relaxing back and wondering at how much difference a year had made in her life. The boys were her joy, her reason for getting up every morning. But now there was more to look forward to than just their shining eyes.

There was Daniel. All the wickedly wonderful ways he made her feel in bed, and the solid caring things she felt outside the bedroom.

She still had some healing to do, but Daniel seemed determined to take his time and give her space when needed. And crowd her at all the right moments, making sure she didn't retreat from moving forward.

Pink-cheeked and relaxed from her bath, she dressed a little fancier than her usual around-the-house getup before making her way downstairs.

"Is it safe to come down?" Beth paused at the base of the landing, not wanting to ruin their surprise.

A flurry of voices called out a warning, and she waited for her escort.

"Don't peek," Nathan warned as they guided her to her chair.

"I wouldn't dream of it." Beth sat cautiously as Lance

moved her chair into place. "Can I look now?"

"Look, look, look..." Robbie was still bouncing when she opened her eyes.

The table was set with a bouquet of flowers in the center, plates arranged around the edges, and over by the stove, Daniel leaned on the counter, all six foot plus of him staring down with contentment on his face. His smile took in the boys as well, and another tendril of warmth uncurled in her belly.

"I made the soup." Robbie crawled into his chair, sitting on his knees as usual.

"Lance got to use the knife but I buttered the bread. You like supper, Mom? You like it?" Nathan carried over a plate covered with grilled cheese sandwiches. She caught the edge before the whole pile slipped to the floor in rush. Beth took a deep breath and *hmm*ed loudly before placing the platter safely on the tabletop.

"I love it. It's wonderful."

So were the cards on her plate she had to read through and admire before any of them could start on the food.

Conversation flowed around the table like only little boys could provide, mouths filled with bites of food chewed rapidly so the next story could be told. Laughter filled the air—Lance had received a heart-shaped card from one of his classmates and been teased about it all the way home on the bus. Nathan was clear in how he'd defend his brother the next time anyone tried something stupid like that again.

Throughout the meal and the cleanup that followed, Beth tried to define what she was feeling. It wasn't until they were sitting in the living room playing a game of snakes and ladders that it hit her.

This was the first Valentine's ever that she'd been given to, instead of doing all the giving.

She held on to the satisfaction and wonder of the sensation through the game and follow-up reading time. Bringing the evening to a close was tough.

"I've had a marvelous evening, boys, and your presents were perfect. Thank you for the wonderful Valentine's Day. But the school bus will be here bright and early, so it's time to say good night to Daniel and hit your pillows."

Groans and complaints died off quick enough when it was clear she was serious.

Robbie crawled beside where Daniel sat on the couch and pulled a slightly tattered piece of paper from behind his back.

"What 'cha you got there, tiger?" Daniel took it and opened it carefully. A bright smile spread across his face. "Well, I think that's about the best Valentine I ever did get."

"I can't draw very good."

"You drew great." Daniel pointed to the page. "What they doing there?"

"The doggies are chasing the deer, like we saw last weekend when you took us on the snowmobile. Can we go again?"

"Course."

"I get to go by myself this time, right?" Lance paused in the middle of cleaning up the game.

Daniel looked over at Beth, hesitating before answering. "Not yet. We ain't got a machine the right size for you to ride solo. You remember I told you that. You'll have to ride double for a while longer."

Lance rolled his eyes and scrambled to his feet, heading for the door.

"Come back and finish cleaning up, please," Beth said firmly.

Her oldest son didn't say a word, but his pointed glances

Daniel's direction were all about showing his displeasure in being treated like a little kid.

Daniel ignored him, instead accepting a big kiss on his cheek from Robbie and a hug from Nathan before the two of them raced away, making car noises en route to their bedroom. Lance left as soon as possible afterward, his nose still out of joint.

Beth held her cup of tea in both hands, rocking as she stared at Daniel.

"Now don't you go apologizing for him or anything." Daniel leaned back and stretched out his legs, ankles crossed easily.

"I wasn't going to. I was going to say thank you for respecting my wishes regarding him riding alone. You didn't have to be the bad guy. You could have said it was my idea."

He shrugged. "No use in us both being in his bad books. You're right, our rides are made for bigger bulk. Unless we get something smaller, it's not safe. I'd probably have forgotten if you hadn't reminded me. I'm not all that up on little-people safety, as you could probably tell by my lack of worry back in the fall with the swimming hole."

Beth got in a leisurely examination as he spoke, eyeing every mouthwatering bit of him. The muscular bulk of his thighs filled his jeans, his strong forearms bared since he'd rolled up his sleeves during dishes and never put them back down. She could almost feel his hands on her body, imagine him stroking with his fingers and bringing her pleasure.

"I like that expression you're wearing, Miss Beth."

She dragged her eyes off the cause of her fantasizing. "You're distracting me."

"Distracting is good."

Beth smiled harder. "I wanted to say thank you for

everything you did tonight. It was very special. The best Valentine's Day ever for me."

If her voice cracked a little on the last word, she thought he could understand.

"I'm glad. I'm only sorry the day can't end the way I'd like it to." Softly spoken, quiet enough the boys couldn't overhear. Lusty and dark enough to make a shiver race over her skin.

"You got time to stay until after I tuck them in?" Maybe they couldn't make love, but sharing and talking—those things were just as important to her soul. Every time they spent together made her more aware of how much she'd grown to care for him. Care about him.

Daniel rose and pulled her to her feet, bringing her flush to his body and holding her close, his chin resting on the top of her head. "I'll stay. You take as long as you need, but I'll be waiting for you here."

That was the miracle. That was the real truth—he would be waiting for her. Beth squeezed him tight, not wanting to let go.

"*Mooom.* Robbie's playing with the toothpaste again."

Daniel snorted. "God, run, don't walk. That's a potential disaster in the making."

He released her toward the stairs. She didn't waste any time because, yeah, the last toothpaste battle was still fresh in her mind. But she did glance over her shoulder before getting out of view.

The fact Daniel was still watching pleased her more than she could possibly explain.

Chapter Twenty

Gabe exited the hardware store and literally bumped into his cousin.

Daniel caught him by the shoulders, steadying them both. "Hey, you want to bounce, try the trampoline at the rec hall."

At that moment, bouncing anything but his fists off a firm surface was the last thing on his mind. Gabe pulled his thoughts away from his lingering exasperation to concentrate fully on Daniel. "I didn't expect to see you for another couple weeks. How's calving going?"

There was a trace of cow shit on Daniel's boots, dark streaks of mud along the cuffs of his jeans. His eyes were tired but he still managed to look insanely happy. "Typical April chaos. I'm in town for fifteen minutes on a supply run before diving back into the fray. You bastard—taking it easy right now, aren't you? Your family did the hard labour back in February. You've got nothing to do but wait for the fields to thaw before seeding."

Waiting. Waiting. That was all Gabe felt he was doing. A sigh escaped before he could stop it. "Yeah, I'm living a life of fucking leisure. I should drop in at the Queen's for tea."

A furrow appeared between Daniel's eyes. "What's wrong?"

"Nothing."

Daniel planted a hand on his shoulder and pushed hard

enough to make Gabe rock on his feet, moving him out of the path of the front doors. "Bullshit. You've been MIA for the past while, and it's not just that you're busy. We're all busy. I still usually see you a few times a month. Spit it out."

Gabe wasn't about to spill the entire story in the middle of the street. "You're extra busy these days. The Coleman rumor mill says your lady keeps you hopping."

The glow of happiness lighting Daniel's face would have made the twist of jealousy in Gabe's gut sharper if he wasn't honestly damn pleased for his cousin.

"Beth is..." Daniel closed his mouth and shook his head, his grin growing wider by the second.

"That good, eh?"

"Better." Daniel pulled himself from his love-struck musings, turning his focus on Gabe again. "You still didn't answer me, though. I know something's happened."

Gabe snorted. "Now you're gonna be a psychiatrist as well as a coach? Isn't it enough that you've changed your life over the past months? Just like you said you would?"

"The plan, if I recall right, was for both of us to change our lives. What happened with all your ideas? Still working on them?"

"You could say that." He'd shared some of his musings with Daniel. It had been nerve racking but positive to bounce ideas off someone else. And now it seemed it was all for nothing.

Comprehension spread slowly over Daniel's face. "Uncle Ben causing you grief?"

It wasn't the time. It wasn't the place. Still, hell if Gabe knew when they'd get a chance to talk, and he really wanted to unload, bad. "You know my dad and I don't see things the same way. He found a bunch of my mail in his mailbox—flyers and shit about the organic stuff I've been researching. He took it as an insult and tore a strip off me. 'The ranch isn't some goddamn experiment for a bunch of granola-eating hippy freaks.' I'm to do as I'm told—like some wet-behind-the-ears schoolboy."

Daniel leaned back against the concrete side of the building. "Damn shame. It sounded like you were on to something."

That was the kicker. "I *am* on to something. I'm not giving up, just...taking it slower."

"But I thought you said—"

Gabe shook his head. "I've gotta step back for a while, it's true. It's not worth pushing him and making things worse, not with Rafe still living at home. And Dad is right—it's officially his land and he is in charge. Doesn't mean I can't do my damnedest to get things ready for the time I can buy him out. Or by some miracle, make him see things in a new light."

Gabe had spent enough time worrying and poking at the problem to know the ranch had to change. But fighting his father and tearing apart his family more by antagonizing the man was counter to part of what he hoped to accomplish. A thriving ranch *and* an intact family.

Didn't make the regrets less that he had to put his dreams aside just as he felt he was making some progress.

Daniel's smile returned, curling his lips and lighting his eyes. "Well, you son of gun. You're doing it."

"Doing what?"

"Meeting the challenge." Daniel poked him in the chest.

Gabe stood there for a moment, wondering what the hell his cousin was talking about. Maybe his brain was still numb from the long winter, because it took the longest time for realization to trickle through as Daniel stared him down, silently waiting for him to put the puzzle pieces together.

Waiting? Motionless? He'd been choked because his delay in plans felt as if he'd gone back to his old drifting ways. The cold pain he'd felt since New Year's deadening his senses. But...this wasn't drifting. It was more like holding back the floodwaters or containing energy in a battery. Storing up the power to release it when it would best be used.

Another thump shook him from his meditations. He blinked hard and concentrated on Daniel. His familiar face was right there, expectation written all over it.

"Damn it, you're right," Gabe confessed.

Daniel raised a brow. "And you say that like it's a total surprise."

Gabe snorted. "Bastard."

"Nope—you know my parents were married. Asshole? I'll accept asshole."

They exchanged grins and slapped each other on the shoulder before pacing in opposite directions, returning to their own tasks.

Their challenge wasn't finished—not for either of them. Daniel, from what he'd seen, was a lot closer to reaching an end. But...that was okay. Moving forward in life wasn't a race to the finish line.

Gabe took a deep breath of the springtime air and headed back to his truck with a far lighter heart than he'd had for a long time.

Chapter Twenty-One

"You need to get down here right now." The frantic tone in Beth's voice came through loud and clear, even through the words were whispered.

Daniel glanced at his watch. Why was she calling him just past one on a school day? She should be in class right now. "Beth? What's the matter? Something happen at work? Are the boys okay?"

She hesitated for a second, and his heart nearly stopped, thinking of all the terrible things that could have happened. "The boys are fine. Jaxi's in labour and..."

He had the truck turned toward the hospital already. "Don't tell me there's something wrong."

"She's doing great. It's a few weeks before her due date, but it's May already so there's no concern. It's your brother who—" Beth lowered her voice again. "Okay, there's no other way to say this, but he's having a little trouble, and I think he needs someone to hold his hand."

The first wave of fear washed away only to be replaced with confusion. "Blake's in trouble? Why's he in trouble if Jaxi's in labour?"

"*Because* Jaxi's in labour? I don't know, Daniel, but I'd appreciate if you got here quickly. Jaxi wants him to stick around, and we think he's on the verge of making for the hills."

Oh hell no, that wouldn't go over well with Jaxi at all. Daniel found his face being split by a huge grin. "I'm on my way. How's Jaxi?"

"Great. She should have the baby in the next couple hours or so if things continue well. The doctors don't seem worried at all, at least not about her. I think they're imagining Blake falling into a faint and cracking his head open on the floor or something."

Oh, the ammunition they were going to have to tease Blake with in the future. "Jaxi have no problem with me joining you in the labour room?"

Beth's sweet laugh stroked him with her delight. "She's kicked out all the interns and spare nurses, but she's the one who said to call you. Said she figured you'd be too busy taunting Blake about being a wuss to be peeking at her privates."

Only Jaxi.

He pulled into the parking lot and headed for the main doors. "I'm nearly there. What floor, and then tell me quick how you're doing, darling."

"Third floor, room four. I'm—I'm so glad I can be here for this. I'm still shocked that Jaxi asked me to help her. It's a little tough, but it's good. And, my God, is Jaxi ever a hoot. Even in labour she's bossing Blake around and cracking jokes. I need to get back. See you soon?"

"In a few minutes."

Daniel tugged off his coat as he ran the stairs. He never thought he'd get to witness a baby's arrival. He'd never thought he'd be called on to make sure his big brother stayed around to see it either.

He wasn't sure which tickled him more.

The staff at the top of the stairs eyed him for all of two seconds before his cousin Tamara stood and pointed the way. "It's the start of a whole new Six Pack generation. We got the phone lines warmed up and ready to spread the news."

"How are the bets standing?"

Tamara laughed. "Boys are the top choice as expected. About eight out of ten figure that way."

Daniel's cheeks hurt from grinning so hard. There was a baby coming, and he was going to get to see his nephew arrive. Or niece. What an incredible twist to his day. He'd helped deliver enough animals over the years he wasn't worried about the messy parts about to happen. It was the miracle of it this time being a tiny person that threatened to blow his mind.

Course he wasn't about to tell his sister-in-law he'd been comparing cows in labour to her about to give birth.

Daniel paused to knock on the door.

The wooden surface swung inward, and Beth's curls bounced into view. She winked and let him in. He stepped forward cautiously, uncertain what he was about to witness.

He didn't expect the scene to involve a very pregnant Jaxi, decked out in a pretty blue robe, holding on to a tall pole that held a contraption with blinking lights. Wires led off the square and disappeared under her robe, but other than that she looked normal. She stood beside what looked to be a La-Z-boy rocker. Blake occupied the chair, stretched nearly flat with his feet raised and head back.

Daniel laughed. "You two got something mixed up from what I remember in the text books."

Jaxi turned to greet him, the edges of her smile tighter than usual. "Hey, you. Did I call you away from something important?"

He crossed the distance between them and wrapped her in a hug. "Nothing more important than this. Don't you worry. I'm here for however long you need and whatever you need me for."

The bulk of her belly pressed him, the pole got in the way, and for a second he wasn't sure where and what he was supposed to touch or not touch. She ignored his discomfort and buried her face against his chest, close for a brief moment before releasing him. She lifted her chin, and he squeezed the fingers she'd slipped into his hand.

"Come on, Jaxi." Beth moved past him to duck under Jaxi's arm and urge her toward the door, the pole rolling along with them. "We can walk the hall for another lap before the doctor gets back to check you."

Jaxi poked out her tongue. "Yes, ma'am. You're a slave driver."

"Of course I am. And since I'm supposed to distract you, I'd love you to tell me another story about the boys when they were growing up. Something embarrassing. Know any more?"

"How about the time Daniel got himself locked in the girls' bathroom at school?"

Oh God. Having Jaxi as a sister-in-law was dangerous. She knew every story worth knowing, having been around for most of their lives. Of course, half the town had the same memories as well, so it wasn't as if he had any deep, dark secrets to keep.

Beth blew him a kiss over her shoulder just before the women exited the room.

There was an extra chair in the corner, so Daniel dragged it over and sat in it backward. He rested his arms along the top rail and stared at Blake.

His brother's eyes were closed.

Daniel snorted. "Glad you're able to relax and take it easy

at a time like this."

"I'm feeling good enough to belt you into tomorrow if I want."

"That's nice. You up for watching your son or daughter arrive?"

"Oh, God." Blake dragged himself upright, a tinge of green under his skin. "Daniel, this is killing me."

"Jaxi seems to be doing well."

"Yeah, except when I'm walking the hall with her, and she stops and does that weird breathing thing and her fingers dig into my arm so hard I know it's got to hurt like the blazes. And suddenly there's these white spots swirling in front of my eyes, and if you tell anyone I'm a wimp, I'll never forgive you."

He tried to wipe the smile from his face, he really did. "You're going to have to threaten at least a half-dozen relatives to achieve silence on this one, one of them your wife. I don't think you'll have much luck there."

Daniel offered his hand and Blake accepted it sheepishly, rising to his feet uneasily. "Thanks for the sympathy."

He pushed Blake in the direction of the attached bathroom. "I feel for you. I do. Got to be nothing worse than having to watch someone you love hurting and not be able to do anything about it."

"Damn right." Blake splashed his face with water.

Daniel leaned on the wall and tried to remember the last time his brother had ever lost control like this. "But you're going to stay and do whatever you need to, right?"

Blake stopped in the middle of patting his face dry and pulled the towel away to frown at Daniel. "Of course, I'm staying. I wouldn't miss this for the world. Only..." He took a big breath and spoke curtly. "If you notice me getting wobbly on my feet, poke me, hard. That should help."

Permission to poke his brother. This got better and better. "No problem. I got you covered."

The door swung open, and Blake hurried across the room to take over for Beth. He brushed a loose strand of hair off Jaxi's face before kissing her tenderly.

Daniel got distracted by Beth making her way to his side. "What's up?" he asked.

"She's 'feeling funny' which is usually woman code for the next stage of the game. You ready?"

"I'll be the one supporting Blake if needed."

She planted a kiss on his cheek just before the room turned into a flurry of activity. The nurse arrived, then another, although not their cousin Tamara, and Jaxi reluctantly crawled on the bed. People checked her, the doctor slipped into the room. There was a lot more commotion and activity than Daniel expected. He watched everything with fascination until his big brother swayed on his feet.

Daniel rushed forward to sling an arm around him. "You okay?"

Blake's face had gone totally white. "Yes. No."

Jaxi slapped her husband on the arm and glared between panting breaths. "Blake Coleman, if you faint, I'll never forgive you."

Daniel laughed out loud. He couldn't hold it in anymore.

A sharp jab in his side was enough to help him stifle his amusement, at least a little. Beth muttered, "You're here to make sure he stays on his feet, not provide us with a laugh track."

The nurse and doctor were in position, voices raised, not in anger but excitement. Daniel didn't pay much attention to what they were saying, instead he alternated between watching the progress of the newest family member, and making sure Blake kept vertical.

The noises shifted from encouragement and hollering to the sturdy cry of a newborn, and a rush of something indescribable hit.

Blake shifted forward, and for one horrible second Daniel thought his brother had passed out. Thankfully, Blake was only moving into position to accept a squalling baby girl into his arms, the hugest grin pasted on his face.

"Well, damn. She's beautiful."

He leaned on the side of the bed, and Jaxi kissed him and their daughter before squeezing her eyes shut. "Oh boy, that was tough."

"Get ready for round two," the doctor warned. Blinking lights and monitors continued as he turned and spoke to the nurses. A flurry of activity followed even as Daniel choked to a stop, and Beth's arms around his waist tightened in surprise.

"Round two?" Daniel gasped, confusion crowding in.

Blake turned and grinned, all traces of his squeamishness vanished. "You didn't think I was freaking out over Jaxi having a baby, did you? She's made me keep the twins a secret for the past four months, and I've been just about ready to burst."

"You two are incredible." Beth snuck past the action and kissed Jaxi's cheek, wiping her forehead. "Only you, Jaxi."

She smiled, more than a little tired. "Hey, a girl's gotta have some fun. Figured the baby pool needed a kick in the teeth."

It took awhile, but when things got moving, they went and did the last bit all over again, with an air of celebration as the second Coleman daughter arrived and proceeded to out-scream her sister.

Beth turned and hugged Daniel tight, hiding her tears from the room as the medical staff finished up all the things they needed to deal with. Daniel cradled her close, brushing her hair and soothing her the best he could without saying a word. It was a bit of heaven to have witnessed this miracle, and a shot of hell to know that he'd never experience the situation for himself.

The room finally quieted until just family remained. Jaxi met Daniel's gaze, and she lifted one of the girls, the one swaddled tight in her arms. She raised a brow but didn't say anything, and he wondered again how she figured things out without anyone telling her.

"Hey, you want a chance to hold the babies, or take off and let Jaxi and Blake have time to themselves?" Daniel wiped a tear from the corner of her eye. "Up to you. Don't feel any need to rush."

Beth's smile was watery but real. "I'd love to hold them."

They moved back to the bedside, and Jaxi handed over one bundle to Beth. She sat and stared at the little girl whose mouth was pulled into a perfect pucker.

Daniel turned toward Blake and laughed. His older brother looked shell-shocked and hopelessly in love at the same time. "You gonna let me have her for a few minutes?"

"What?" Blake peeled his gaze off the baby and shook himself alert. "Oh, right."

He passed over the tiny bundle, stroking a finger over the newborn's cheek before turning to Jaxi and hugging her, his mouth went close to her ear as they spoke quietly together.

Daniel carried his precious burden over to sit next to Beth. The warm bundle wiggled until he settled her tighter against him. "Shh. You'd better get used to being cuddled because there's an awful lot of people who are going to want to love on you."

To hold a newborn, sitting beside the woman he loved—Daniel sighed with happiness and regret. For the things he couldn't change that were a part of his life, for the things he knew he could do something about. He turned from admiring the dark-haired beauty in his arms to make sure Beth was okay.

She was staring back. Her eyes were huge, tears hovering there. But it wasn't pain or regret, but something rich and meaningful beyond his wildest dreams.

"They're beautiful, aren't they?"

He didn't trust himself to speak. Just nodded. Reached out and draped an arm around her shoulders and pressed his lips to her forehead and kissed her.

Love had been born that day—and he didn't begrudge his brother his good fortune one bit because there was too much love in his own heart. Daniel felt ready to burst with it.

It was time to let Beth know. To make sure she felt the same way about him. For them to be a family as well. Maybe not one by blood and birth, but one by choice. A choice that was as real as the babies resting in their arms.

Chapter Twenty-Two

"You got everything under control?" Daniel tapped Matt on the shoulder as he placed the steak platter beside him.

Matt shrugged. "It's not rocket science. I have done this before, you know."

His brother turned his back on the noise and celebrating coming from the yard, suddenly intent on scrubbing the racks of the barbecue to shiny clean. Daniel sighed then headed back to the house for the rest of the utensils.

Since Helen had taken off, Matt had been—well, not moping, but not the enthusiastic man Daniel was used to seeing. He'd tried digging to find out what exactly had happened, but Joel and Matt both refused to say anything except Helen was gone for good.

He didn't need more details than the hurt he saw in Matt's eyes. Helen would find a damn cold reception if she ever showed her face around Rocky again.

In the meantime, there were plenty of other things to distract him. Joel and Jesse were back from another semester of school, living in the basement rooms at his mom and dad's. He and Matt had moved out. The Six Pack Ranch had invested in a couple of trailers to use for extra living quarters—it was one thing to have the room available in the big house but Matt had insisted, and Daniel had to agree, they were too old to be under their ma and dad's roof anymore. And since none of them were rushing to push Beth and the boys out...

He swung to admire them. The kids ran in circles, screaming in wild delight as Jesse chased them with a super-powered water pistol. Joel filled water balloons to provide retaliation ammunition, and everywhere there was laughter and smiles. Blake carried one of the baby girls in a sling on his chest. Jaxi wore the other as the two of them sat and chatted quietly with the folks and Beth, all of them waiting for the meat to be done. Everywhere he looked he saw family.

Even Travis had made himself available for the annual family May Victoria Day picnic, although he looked a touch uncomfortable with the sudden increase in small people attending the party.

He snuck up to Daniel's side. "I got your rides ready for you, if you're still determined to do this."

Daniel smacked him on the shoulder. "Idiot."

Travis grinned. "Hey. Serious? I'm happy for you."

They stood for a minute, Daniel looking his younger brother over. "I've been pretty lucky, haven't I?"

"Like you've got horseshoes up your ass."

A laugh burst out. "There you go. Now you just need to get yourself kicked and you too can be so fortunate."

Travis shook his head. "No rush. I'm happy getting things settled around here with you taking over the shop. I certainly don't need any rug rats tying me up or tying me down."

"Your loss. But first I have to get her to actually agree to anything."

"You don't move very fast, do you?"

Daniel gave him the finger. They finished getting everything together for the meal, bringing out the food from the kitchen, hauling out drinks. Chaos of the best sort reigned for the next hour as dinner passed, the outdoor seating filled with squirming boys and family.

He snuck away as soon as he spotted dessert being served. He'd arranged for Beth to join him while the kids were distracted. It was a damn good thing Travis had already saddled their horses—it was scary how much his hands shook. Daniel patted Thunder and Ruffles, and considered his options again, coming to the same conclusion. Even if he felt like a total chickenshit, it was time.

He led the horses outside, tying the reins to the railing, ready to fetch Beth from the festivities. When he turned, she was already halfway down the path, a straw hat in her hand and pretty new boots on her feet.

"Damn, maybe you want to be a cowgirl instead of a teacher. You look mighty fine."

"You sweet talker." She kissed him so thoroughly he had to adjust himself before leading her around the gate.

"You've made this ride far more painful than it should be."

"Me? Little innocent me?" Beth batted her lashes.

"Innocent. Bah." He paused. "You sure you're good riding?"

She nodded. "I've been doing my exercises, and I have been out with Marion a few times. As long as we're not doing anything fancy, my leg can take it."

He helped her mount before swinging himself up and leading them into the field. They followed the course of the creek to where it joined the river, the waters high with spring runoff. Laughter surrounded them as she told him the latest stories about her students, the final exam nerves hitting hard as the school year wound down. Their ride was easy and peaceful, and felt oh-so-right to be together.

"You happy to be teaching again next year?"

"Very. I like the school, and the kids on the whole were great. I think a couple more years will work fine. I don't know that I want to be teaching when Lance hits my grade, but there's enough time to worry about that later."

Daniel grinned. "Lance. Headstrong doesn't even begin to describe him."

"You should talk." Beth's shining face made his heart sing. Yes, it was time. He leaned over and took hold of her reins, slowing Ruffles to a standstill. "Daniel, if you've got something funny planned for us while I'm sitting on a horse, I'm afraid I'm not that kinky."

"Well, shoot." He brushed his lips against hers, then led Ruffles and Thunder to the side. "Here I was thinking a little rodeo clown handstand routine would be one of our next experiments."

He dismounted and tethered their mounts before reaching to grab her. The horses lowered their heads, pulling new grass happily as Beth crawled off. He slipped an arm under her legs, ignoring her cry of surprise as he carried her toward the tree overlooking the river.

"You're not thinking of—?"

"Nothing unusual. Just relax." He could have let her walk, but he wanted to hold her.

She softened in his grasp, nuzzling his neck. "I haven't been out this direction before. Your mom took me to the east, and the north."

"The river is one of the favourite viewpoints for the entire family. But I asked her to let me have this privilege. To show you myself."

A small crease appeared between her brows. "Now you've gone all mysterious on me."

Daniel slowed. "You'll understand soon enough."

He let her down. He held his breath as she stepped forward, turning slowly to take in the panorama.

"Daniel, this is beautiful. The view—the river is amazing…"

She glanced at him then walked away, headed for the base of the huge cottonwood. There was a bench tucked up to the trunk, the solid legs, the smooth arms of the sturdy construction protected by layers of marine varnish to keep it sound in spite of being out under the elements. Beth smiled over her shoulder, stroking the wood with a flowing touch, approval in her motions.

"You made this, didn't you?" she asked, turning back to admire it further.

He knew the second she spotted the plaque. The tightness in her body wasn't fear, wasn't her about to run, but he wondered if he'd pushed too hard.

Beth turned to face him, her eyes filled with moisture, lips quivering as they drew into a smile that fought to win over her tears. "Oh, Daniel."

He came to her side and sat them on the bench. She traced the words with a fingertip. *Baby Laurie. Held in our hearts forever.*

"I wanted you to have something to remember her by. I wanted you to have a place to know that all the good things in your past are not forgotten."

She lowered her head to her hands and sobbed. His eyes grew watery as he curled an arm around her shoulders and held her. A breeze floated up from the water, the fresh scent of green growing things mixed with the richness of the earth and the wild flowers in bloom. Everything around them was alive and bursting with the promise of coming summer.

When her crying slowed, he reached into his pocket and brought out the wad of tissue he'd placed there, anticipating it might be needed.

She drew a shaky breath. "Thank you."

Daniel gave her time to wipe and dry, brushing away his own tears as he settled back farther on the bench.

She snuggled against his side, laying her head on his shoulder. "I can't tell you how much this means to me. Really, I can't."

"Don't have to say anything. I understand."

They looked over the river, leaves and small twigs floating past, escaping from view around the corner. Beth sighed, a content and peaceful sound. Daniel felt a smile come to his face.

"Daniel?"

"Hmm?"

She didn't move, just clung to his arm as they stared into the sunshine. "Will you marry me?"

Daniel jerked, dislodging her from his shoulder. "What?"

She turned to face him fully. "I know, it's unusual, but I figured I started this relationship way back when, but when we slowed down last December..."

Her voice trailed off, her smile getting bigger by the minute.

"Say it again." Daniel cupped her chin in hand, letting the joy inside him bubble up. "I want to hear it again."

Beth sparkled. There was no other word for it. "I love you, Daniel Coleman. Every bit of you, from that long hard body that makes me shake with pleasure to the tender things you say and do. I want you to be my husband. To share my life with me. To be far, far more than just a good time."

Daniel laughed and picked her up in his arms, squeezing

her tight as he kissed her silly. When they finally let each other go, there was still a question on her face. "What? You need me to say it?"

"Oh, yes."

He shook his head. "You realize that's why I brought you out here today? Not only to show you the bench but to propose."

Beth covered her mouth with her fingers. "Oh dear, I didn't mean to ruin your surprise."

"Ruin it? Hell, you couldn't possibly ruin anything." Daniel held her chin, unable to stop from dropping another kiss on her lips. "Miss Beth? I would love to marry you. You're exactly what I want in my life, and in my bed. And yes, we are far more than just a good time together."

They were both grinning like fools. He brushed the remainder of a tear from her cheek, amazed to be so full inside. Happiness he'd never imagined was his.

"So...you want to go house hunting?" Daniel was ready to drag her into town this minute.

"Today?"

His excitement poured out. "Well, I've already been looking at a few places, just in case you were silly enough to say yes."

Beth squeezed his fingers. "Good. Then you'll be happy to know I've been looking at places as well."

"Really?"

"Really. In case you were silly enough to accept *my* proposal."

Daniel brought her to her feet and headed them toward the horses. "I love I get to brag that you asked."

She shook her head in disbelief. "You're going to brag about that?"

"Damn right, I am."

He helped her up on Ruffles. She frowned for a moment. "You serious? About looking at houses right now?"

"Why not?" He wanted to shout to the world that she was his, but they'd have to take it quieter for the boys' sake. The house was a logical first step.

Beth considered. "Fine, but I need to stop by your place first."

The ride back to where he'd put his trailer went quick enough. Daniel tethered the horses before letting her in, slapping her on the butt as she snuck past him. "Don't take too long."

She stuck out her tongue then sashayed toward the bathroom. He wandered into the kitchen and poured a glass of water, chugging it back as he waited. They could find a place, maybe even get moved in this summer. August wedding before school started...

"Daniel, I need a hand."

He headed down the hall to rescue her. "You can't be lost. And it's too small a bathroom to—*holy fuck*."

Marriage proposals were not supposed to be commemorated by house hunting. Or least, not in her opinion. Beth had learned a lot of lessons from Daniel over the past year, and this was the time for making a memory, all right. Something other than driving the streets of Rocky Mountain House, no matter how excited that thought made her.

There were other ways to celebrate.

Beth stripped as fast as she could before moving to stand stark-naked in the middle of his bedroom doorway and calling for him. She had her back turned, glancing over her shoulder in what she hoped was a sultry come-hither way.

From the expression on his face when he rounded the corner? All thoughts of houses had vanished.

"We should take advantage of the fact the kids are busy. We can take them house hunting with us later."

Daniel's feet were already moving, his T-shirt on the floor and his belt unbuckled. "Damn right. You're more than a pretty face, ain't you, darling?"

"Damn right," she echoed back. Then she was headed toward his bed, crowded by his hard body and his heated grasp. He turned her, arms cradling her, his jeans falling to the floor as he kicked his feet free and joined her on the mattress, naked flesh to naked flesh.

She'd gotten over her aversion to sex on her back because with Daniel, none of it was boring. Actually, none of it was less than spectacular. All those firm muscles over her, leaning in close, pinning her to sheets as he took her mouth in a kiss that promised an exceptionally wild session.

Bring it on.

Her head was spinning by the time Daniel let her breathe, only to have gasp after gasp escape as he worked his way down her body, sucking her nipples, biting the sides of her breasts. His hands teased and tormented, slipping over her belly, parting her curls and stirring the passion in her core before he'd even slipped a finger in.

He stroked with deceiving indolence, leaning on one elbow to stare into her face as his fingers pierced her, the heel of his hand rubbing so perfectly the orgasm building didn't have time to hover, or hesitate, or any of those things. Her body jolted, arching involuntarily as he maintained the pace and added a nip to her breast.

"God, so good."

"Just the beginning," he whispered back.

The beginning of forever. Beth allowed the first flush of tension to fade because she knew more was coming. One roll brought her on top, happy that the muscles in her hip accepted the stretch as she straddled him.

"Yeah, I like a little cowgirl in the bedroom as well as outside."

Daniel cupped her breasts as she slowly rocked, finding a comfortable position, or as comfortable as she could get with him encouraging her along with more sexy words, more tugs on her body that made breathing difficult. His shaft lay in the valley between her legs, each pass rubbing his heat over her clit and sending her higher.

"That's it, darling. Put your hands on me and touch me."

Beth obeyed, reaching down to surround his cock and caress it. Rub the sticky seed escaping from the head and press her fingers like a sheath to enfold him tightly. Daniel groaned with pleasure, his head falling back, hands dropping to her hips. She was tempted to slide back even more and cover him with her mouth. Suck him deep and let him enjoy her that way.

She wanted it all, wanted to give him everything. When he adjusted her, one hand grabbing his cock and directing the head into her, it was too soon and yet...

"Oh God, *yes.*"

One slow slide together. Her moving down, him lifting up. An incredible sense of fullness struck as they briefly rested together.

Her body, her heart. Her soul—all of her loved and cherished like she'd never experienced before.

Daniel smiled, cupping her cheek and drawing her closer to join their lips as he took control of the tempo. Thrusting lazily, an intriguingly lovely twist to his hips that ensured she felt the motion to the tips of her toes. His tongue stroked her teeth, brushed her lips, his kisses flitted across her cheek until he'd buried his face against her neck and bit lightly. He slipped his hands lower, caressing her hips, grip possessive over her ass.

The rhythm never faltered. Made her hotter, made her crazy. Again and again he drove them together. She buried her hands in his hair and squeezed everything she had inside.

Daniel gasped against her skin. She smiled and did it again, and this time the extra pressure set them both off, his hips jerking under her as he strove to get deeper. Clutching her ass as if he were melding them into one. Her body luxuriated in the bliss soaking her limbs. There was nowhere to go but straight down into a puddle of muscleless satisfaction as she lay draped over him.

His heart pounded for the longest time, keeping time with hers.

"Wow."

Daniel laughed. "So you can still speak. I wasn't sure I could."

Beth manoeuvred her way upward by bracing her hands on his chest. She stared at his familiar features, the firm line of his jaw, the steady gaze in his eyes. His face revealed so much more than the initial physical attraction she'd felt—it showed his character, his patience. His raw sexuality, and his love.

She had forever to enjoy him. To trust him. It wasn't a bad place to start.

Chapter Twenty-Three

Daniel pulled in front of the hardware shop with his dad riding shotgun just as Beth exited, two of the boys in tow. All three of them had their arms full of paint cans and brushes.

"I'll stay in the truck," Mike offered. "Go help your damsel in distress."

Daniel hurried over to take her armload.

"Where's Lance?" he asked. Nathan and Robbie dumped their supplies into the back of his truck and swung over the edge to sit in the open box. "Hey, guys. What do think you're doing?"

Nathan popped up, both arms wrapped around one of the ranch dogs. "We wanna ride back here."

Daniel hid his smile and jerked his thumb forward. "In the cab."

"Awwww…" They complained but they moved, crawling through the open split window to land in puddles on the crew cab seat. Daniel chuckled until he glanced back to see Beth watching him with a raised brow.

"What? I don't mind if they get in the cab that way. Better than thinking they get to ride in the back with the dogs."

She shook her head. "You're such a male."

He leaned over and nibbled on her ear. "You were glad of that last night, Miss Beth."

"Very."

They held each other close, and Daniel counted his blessings like he had every damn day for the past six months.

Beth tugged on his hips. "Lance needs help. He can't make up his mind, and I think he's driving the clerk insane."

"Really? Lance always seems to know exactly what he wants. And what he doesn't want."

"Well, this time there's trouble. Come on, I think you'll find it interesting." She walked with him toward the door, her smile blindingly bright.

Daniel made his way into the store about to burst with curiosity.

Waiting to get to know each other better before doing anything formal with their relationship had been the best thing he and Beth could have done. They had no doubts that more than being lovers, they were friends.

But it was the way the boys had slowly come around that made them both the happiest. Nathan accepted the idea of Daniel the fastest, maybe because he was the first to open up to Daniel and talk about his father. Little Robbie never said anything much, just crawled into Daniel's lap one day and kissed him straight out before kissing Beth and toddling off to bed.

Lance was the holdout. Still watching, still judging. Now that they were getting the house in town ready for moving in together, the kid seemed to finally be coming to a decision about the whole deal.

Daniel was worried it wasn't going to be pretty. Lance reminded him a lot of himself at that age. Stubborn but quiet. The kind you couldn't move without a bulldozer unless he decided to give way.

Lance had both clerks trapped, cans of paint and wallpaper swatches littering the countertop. One of them spotted Daniel and relief showed in the man's eyes.

"Look, someone to help you decide. I'll be over here when you're ready." Both attendants fled.

Daniel laughed. "Lance, what are you doing? You've got more coloured bits of paper on the counter than there are jellybeans in the candy shop."

Lance snorted. "As if."

"So what's the trouble? I thought you had an idea picked out already."

"It was too girly."

Sweet Jesus, here they went with the girly business again. Wait until the kid realized the female sex didn't have cooties. He was going to be a handful. "You want horses?"

"Nope."

"Race Cars?"

"Nope."

"Circus clowns, elephants and balloons?" Daniel thought that one would make the kid take notice. Lance grimaced in disgust.

"I'm not a baby."

"No, you ain't." Daniel leaned on the counter and poked at the papers. "Seems to me most of these are a little on the young side for you. Tell you what, the room you picked out pretty much just needs a fresh coat of paint, then you can add the things you want over the next while."

Lance stared in suspicion. "I thought we had to get everything ready for moving in a couple of weeks."

Beth stepped closer and Daniel wrapped an arm around her, pulling her tight to his side. She felt so good in his arms, so right, and he couldn't resist stopping to drop a kiss on her cheek. She smiled, one hand behind his back, the other resting on his chest.

Lance checked every move they made.

"We have to be able to shift your furniture in, that's true. But there's no way that at the end of the day we're going to have everything the way we want it forever. In fact, that's one of the fun parts—you get to keep changing things and making things to show off your interests. Find what you love to do, and suddenly there's all kinds of projects you'll want to put in your room."

"Like the stuff you make?"

Daniel nodded. "Yeah, I suppose."

"You think I could make something in the workshop for my room?"

"Course you could. With supervision, but I'd love to help you."

Lance cracked a smile and pointed at the paint samples. "Which one?"

Daniel checked them out and pulled three to the side. "If you're going to make some furniture, pick your favourite of these. They're neutral enough to look good for a long time." He leaned over. "And they are not the least bit girly."

Lance checked them over slowly then picked one up. "This one."

"Give it to the man, and he'll mix it for you." Daniel watched the boy track down the clerk. He turned back to Beth who was smiling, a twinkle in her eye. "What was that all about?"

"He didn't like my suggestions," Beth said. "I pointed out almost the same things you did, but he didn't trust me."

"Hell, no, you're a girl. You might contaminate his room."

Beth poked him in the chest and he laughed.

The clerk cleared his throat. "Excuse me, I need to make sure you approve this before I tint the paint."

"My dad said that was the best one. He's going to help me make things for my room too." Lance glanced up at Daniel. "Right?"

Daniel's heart leapt into his throat, and beside him Beth's hands squeezed his arm painfully hard. Did Lance even realize what he'd said? The word had popped out so casually.

"Right."

Daniel looked just about everywhere in the shop for the next five minutes as the paint shook in the machine, fighting to keep his emotional high from showing. Dancing in the aisles seemed like a marvellous idea, but it might freak a few people out.

Every bit of his world was finally coming together.

The fire crackled, the sound mixing with the other familiar noises of the big old house. Beth leaned on Daniel's chest, cuddled between his thighs as they both stared into the flickering flames. The boys were camping for the night with a couple of their soon-to-be-official uncles, Jesse and Joel. She wondered if the twins realized how little sleep the boys were planning.

"I'm going to miss this house." Beth stroked her hand along his leg, tracing circles with her fingertip. There were good memories tied up in the place. The kids laughing, schoolwork getting done. Everyday living that somehow felt that much richer now. Deeper.

Safer.

"You'll be able to come and visit as often as you like since Jaxi and Blake are moving in with the girls."

She laughed. "I still can't believe Jaxi kept the twins a secret her entire pregnancy."

"I can't believe Blake made it through the delivery."

They grinned at each other.

"It's as if this house has a revolving door. How do you decide who gets what?" She'd always thought she'd hit the jackpot when she'd been offered the place.

Daniel rubbed her shoulders, running his fingers through the short hair of her neckline. "Whoever needs it the most, I guess. My dad took over the main ranch house since he was the oldest, and for a lot of years this place had one set or another of my uncles and aunts and cousins living here. Now they're all scattered around the area. Some built houses on the sections of the land they own, some moved elsewhere because they decided to get into something other than ranching."

"Like you."

"Like me...and you."

They were moving in together, they were getting married. She'd put off the one last thing they needed to do. She pivoted in his arms. Twisting was much easier than a year ago, the flexibility and range of motion in her limb nearly back to one hundred percent.

"Daniel, I want to..." His sexy smile distracted her for long enough he leaned in and kissed her.

Kissed her thoroughly, taking her mouth and lips by storm and turning the gentle caress into something on the hot and needy side. She dragged back with reluctance. "Whoa, cowboy, I want to do that too, but first we need to talk about something else."

He stoked her cheek and rearranged her in his lap so she could lean back on his legs. "We've gotten good at talking, as well as the sexin'. What's on your mind?"

She took a big breath. "What do you think about making the wedding a joint celebration?"

Confusion painted his face. "Who else you know that wants to get married?"

She shook her head. "No, I meant...if you'd like...if you think you're ready..."

"Spit it out already woman, I'm dying here."

"Do you want to adopt the boys?"

Pure, unadulterated joy leapt into his eyes. "You mean it?"

It was exactly the response she'd hoped for. The kind of response she'd expected. With every action over the past months, Daniel had shown time and time again he wanted only the best for her, and the boys. "I think they're all ready for the idea, and isn't that kind of what you're getting? A wife and kids? Let's make it official."

Daniel dropped his head back, but not before she spotted the tears in his eyes.

"I love them too, you know. Kinda crept up and swallowed me whole, even when I was trying to not hope for anything." He clasped her chin in his hand, his thumb reaching to brush her bottom lip in a tender caress. "Falling in love with you has changed my entire life. I don't know what I would have done if you hadn't come dancing into my world."

"Stumbling in, more like it."

"I caught you."

She kissed his thumb as it passed by. "You did, and you held on until my world stopped shaking. Until I was able to stand alone."

"But you're not alone, Miss Beth, you got me. Forever and ever."

She drew him to the carpet, and they made love. Slow and sweet, everything she had wanted for years and years, and it was because they were friends and lovers.

They were everything important. They were family.

About the Author

Vivian Arend has hiked, biked, skied and paddled her way around most of North America and parts of Europe. Throughout all the wandering in the wilderness, stories have been planted and they are bursting out in vivid colour. Paranormal, twisted fairytales, red-hot contemporaries—the genres are all over.

Between times of living with no running water, she home schools her teenaged children and tries to keep up with her husband—the instigator of most of the wilderness adventures.

She loves to hear from readers: vivarend@gmail.com. You can also drop by www.vivianarend.com for more information on what is coming next.

He's the one who taught her to ride.
Now all he wants is to ride her.

Rocky Mountain Heat
© *2011 Vivian Arend*
Six Pack Ranch, Book 1

Blake Coleman is old enough to know that acting on impulse causes nothing but a heap of trouble. But when trouble's a western-hat-wearing blonde with slim legs that go on forever, what's a man to do? Wanting the sweet girl next door is just wrong. The responsible thing to do is keep his hands off.

Jaxi has other plans for Blake's hands, and his heart. She may have once considered him a big brother, but that was a long time ago. She's all grown up now and ready to convince him that she's perfect for him. Except he can't seem to see past the big "don't touch" sign that's apparently still hanging around her neck.

When Jaxi ends up living right under Blake's nose, the undeniable heat between them slides off simmer and leaps up to barn-burning levels. However, a few of the younger six-pack Colemans have decided Jaxi's brand of trouble is worth risking a few busted bones.

That is, if Blake's finally ready to let go the reins and fight for what he wants...

Warning: Sexy cowboys seducing and being seduced in trucks, pool halls and barns. Droolworthy country charm, a little double-teaming, a few secrets and a whole lot of brothers to look forward to. Anyone wanna go for a ride?

Available now in ebook and print from Samhain Publishing.

She wants it. He's got it. And the chase is on...

Chasin' Eight
© 2011 Lorelei James
Rough Riders, Book 11

Bull rider Chase McKay has finally landed in a pile too big to charm his way out of. Caught with his pants down, he finds himself bucked right off the PBR tour until he can get his act together.

Hollywood actress Ava Cooper became the tabloids' favorite target when her longtime boyfriend was outed as gay. Now she wants a place to lay low and a chance to prove to herself that she can satisfy a red-blooded man between the sheets. The sexy, rugged cowboy she finds holed up in her Wyoming hideaway seems like the answer to her every fantasy.

But Chase has sworn off women. Forever. Or at least a month. Whichever comes first.

When they take to the road to get Chase more hands-on bull riding experience, they have every intention of keeping their hands off each other. But the two headstrong stars quickly end up riding a hot and heady rodeo circuit all their own—until the press gets wind of their affair. When the dust clears and the lights of the paparazzi fade, are they ready to give up chasing the dream for a chance of finding forever?

Warning: Strap in, another hot McKay is about to bust out of the gate and this bull rider knows a thing or two about riding hard...

Available now in ebook and print from Samhain Publishing.

PUBLISHING

www.samhainpublishing.com

Green for the planet.
Great for your wallet.

It's all about the story...

Romance

HORROR

www.samhainpublishing.com

CPSIA information can be obtained at www.ICGtesting.com
Printed in the USA
LVOW06s0953230214

374822LV00001B/209/P